SEEDS

Part One of The Grapefruit Tree

A Novel in Four Parts

Bryan Moon

The author would like to acknowledge the financial assistance given to him by the Banff Centre and the Ontario Arts Council.

ISBN 0 88750 701 8 (hardcover)
ISBN 0 88750 702 6 (softcover)

Cover art by Egon Schiele.
Book design by Michael Macklem

Printed in Canada

PUBLISHED IN CANADA BY OBERON PRESS

For R.W.M.

There must have been some precise point when the itchy, cotton-swathed silence of late afternoon became the clear, bell-like silence of early evening, but I could never identify it. By 3.30, the heat would have driven everyone inside. We were reading, talking quietly or simply lying on sofas or beds, half asleep as the curtains billowed out, pressing against the screens. The only sound we heard from outside was the occasional departure of some farmer in his pickup truck. It did not matter what his errand had been or who he was; all that mattered was the clamour of the truck's passage. Each vehicle that went by made a whole townful of hot, rattling, clanging sound. Then, perhaps, no further sound would be heard for a half-hour; we would begin to relax, maybe even doze. Suddenly we would be brought awake again as another vehicle exploded over the series of potholes in front of Mr. Barstow's shop.

It was like trying to go to sleep in a wind storm. No sooner do you begin to fade than another gust hits the house and creaks the rafters, making you wonder if the roof needs re-shingling or the garbage cans are still upright. For a time you try to discern some regularity in the gusts that will help you to sleep, but after a while you give up and simply wait for the next onslaught. Then, as soon as you decide the gusts have stopped and begin to relax, they come again.

Finally, when we had given up counting, the last truck would leave town, and all who were listening would welcome the clamour with a final and vengeful acceptance of noise and heat. We would listen to it run all the way out of town, over the last pothole and the last culvert, until the noise was only a faint echo in our imaginations. Then, still holding onto that after-taste of sound, we would come out of our hot, dusty hypnosis, one by one, and cautiously open blinds or shades or curtains to peek out, fully expecting a further outbreak to welcome the venture. Someone, perhaps Miss Genge from next door, would step out onto the front porch. With the carrying tones of someone calling back to shore from thigh-deep in some summer vacation lake, we would hear her voice, "It's not so bad out here, Edith. Colin, come on out."

It could be that the whole town heard her, because one by one, up and down the street, people would begin to emerge. Mr. Macphail

5

from across the street and down three houses would step out of his front door, his skinny legs made even more thin and bony by his out-sized khaki shorts. Draped over his shoulder, a cross between a beach towel and a toga, would be a bright red-and-green hammock. He would walk to his front gate and look up and down the street, as if to quell any laughter about his skinny legs, and then return to the front corner of his house and string the hammock there between the wall and a poplar. Perhaps he might stop and talk to Mrs. Rose who would be pouring the remainder of her afternoon tea on the flowerbed. We would hear their voices in the still empty street.

Other voices would be heard, calling out from porch to porch or admonishing sons and daughters who could be heard talking and laughing on their way to Main Street. The ceremonial clinking of ice cubes in pitchers of iced tea would be heard. The slap of screen-doors would increase in frequency. Still, however, there was a slight hurrying in the figures on the street, a tuning-up note in the sounds they made, because while the hot afternoon had ended, nightfall had yet to take its place.

Then a pickup truck, possibly the same one that was the last to leave two or three hours earlier, would be heard approaching Union. Once again the town would focus upon the sound; now approaching, it came in reverse order from the afternoon as the truck came back over the bridge, the culverts and the railroad tracks in turn. Instead of reminding everyone of the heat, it now brought the promise of real nightfall.

Many voices would begin to rise. Every voice was telling a story, and Bobby and I heard it happen so many nights and from so many locations as we wandered the town that I think we heard them all. From verandahs and porches, from patios, from opened car windows, from in front of the Café, from beside the hotel, from behind the hardware, from parked cars on the bluff, from beneath the yard light at the school grounds, from every corner and cleared space where someone sat released from the heat of the day, Bobby and I would hear a voice rise, sending a story up into the darkness so that it seemed a river of sound was flowing over Union.

I believe that it is possible they were all parts of the same story, so

6

that if you could listen from the right vantage point, perhaps the right distance in time, you could hear the whole story complete for the first time. They say that radio waves travel out into space forever and that somewhere words said 50 years ago are still echoing. The same could be true of simple voices. Perhaps the echo of the echo of those nights in Union can still be heard deep in the night sky so that right now, in the present, the story is still being told.

I know that I can still hear it. Although it makes no more or no less sense than memory or time, if I listen intently I can hear all of the voices together, and I can hear each one separately. It seems to me that it is all taking place even now, distilled by time into a simple, comprehensible, present tense.

It always begins with my grandfather. He is always the first to hear the night approach in the rattle of the pickup truck as it nears Union. He stands up and walks to the railing of the verandah. He stands tensely, in an attitude of listening.

"Could be the Arnson boy. Arnson's truck has needed new shocks since Christmas." He listens again. "Or it could be George Franklin with that Chevy of his. If he gears down for the bridge it's Arnson, and if not then it's George Franklin." Bobby and I can see him right above us. We are sitting at the base of the grapefruit tree, and he is leaning out over the railing.

From behind him we hear another voice. Disregarding his nightly guessing game about the owners of approaching vehicles, or perhaps joining in after her own fashion, my grandmother is speaking. "Heat is like a big snow..." She is speaking to Jennifer who has come over for tea, or maybe even Jerome Barstow, or perhaps just to the approaching night. "It covers you like a blanket. Curious how it seems to bring memories. You wake up the morning of a big snow and everything outside is gone.... Takes me a full hour to do the morning dishes because the window catches me like a hen on a crossed line.... I just stare out. After five minutes I am not even looking at the snow anymore. After all, there's nothing to see. So I look inside and remember other storms. Then I wake up later with my hands in cold dishwater.... Heat does the same thing. It wraps you up in closed curtains and you start to look inside.... Today I

7

was remembering another hot month like this...Nineteen twenty-two..."

Grandfather stiffens with suppressed impatience. He breaks into the pause of Grandmother's story. "It could be the Peacock boy. He is moving pretty fast. Ha. He is always a little late when he goes to call on Jeanie Sthol, and by gawd, there is one young lady who won't wait for anyone very long." The "ha" he calls out rings false. And there is a false heartiness in his voice. I look up at him closely. He is illuminated by a paper lantern that hangs above and behind him, attached to a cord at the top of the verandah. Two years ago he decided that Union was becoming drab, and he ordered two cartons of Festive Japanese Lanterns from a company in Milwaukee. As an advertisement he placed three of them along the verandah—green, yellow and red—much against Grandmother's complaints that they were gaudy and cheap looking. But the advertisement worked, because on this night, from patios, porches and verandahs all over town, paper lanterns wink down. In the daytime they are faded, wrinkled globes of crêpe paper, the little colour left unfaded by the sun has run with the rain and the dew. But with the night they become truly festive. The lantern he stands beneath was red, but now the light it casts is pink, almost violet. It strikes him from above and behind, changing his face into a deeply shadowed mask that is sad in a strangely formal way. That formality clashes with his voice as he once more takes up the guessing game. "What do you figure Ruby? The Peacock boy? Arnson's son?"

But Grandmother is not listening to him or the approaching vehicle. She is collecting her thoughts. She is probably not even aware that she has been interrupted or, if it is all the same story, perhaps it has not been an interruption. "It was hot like this that summer. That winter we had three big snows. We had hot and cold that year. All the children were gone that summer except for John. ... Seemed like the house echoed all that year with the heat and the cold. And you echo with it.... It is curious how hot and cold get mixed up. What was that game we played when I was young? Let me see... Oh yes. There was some sort of mumbo-jumbo and then they would touch the back of your hand...no, the back of your neck, *with an ice cube. But you didn't know it was ice and it felt like flame. Imagine. Such games at courting age.... Now what was it they said before they touched your neck...?" The silence lengthens, and Grandfather glances behind him to where Grandmother is sitting. Some of the tension in his posture and face begins to subside.*

Another voice speaks in the silence. Jennifer-Rose takes up the story. Perhaps she is far up the street, sitting on her back porch and talking to Mr. Houghton who has walked her home from the hotel, and Bobby and I are sitting in the dew-wet grass at the side of the house listening to her. Or perhaps she is sitting on the verandah with my grandmother.

"It's funny about echoes. I mean it is curious about them." She must be sitting on the verandah because when she is with my grandmother her diction always becomes a bit more formal, as if she were sitting with one of her old school teachers. "It is curious about echoes on a night like this. My mother used to say that on a night like this I couldn't hear her call from the house to the barn, but I could hear a dance starting up 30 miles away. And I could always hear Robert coming. He drove that old '36 Dodge. I was just like Mr. Caldwell there. I could hear that car coming clear across the valley, ten miles away. I knew a lot about cars and trucks then. After I started to go out with him I started watching and listening, and I picked up what I could so I could talk to him. He loved working on cars. He always said that he was going to get his mechanic's licence and work in the city. Well. Never mind about that. I remember when he came to get me I would hear him come down Swenson's hill because the Dodge always backfired two or three times on the way down. That has something to do with the compression, but he always said he did it on purpose so I would be ready when he got there. I would have been ready anyways. I have never cared for those who make you wait. Dad used to make a joke. 'But soft, whose voice do I hear from yonder valley?' He meant the backfires. I always laughed." She pauses, perhaps hearing the laughter or waiting to hear it.

"I guess it wasn't all that funny, but it doesn't ever hurt to laugh. Dad was always uneasy about Robert. It was just one of

9

those little jokes you use the same way you might say 'Hello, how are you?' It's like that when I work the dining-room over supper. Fred Lowe always says, 'Give me some of that special banana cream pie for dessert, Jennifer.' And we laugh. What happened is that when I first started there I gave him lemon meringue by mistake. So now when he wants lemon meringue, he asks for banana cream, and when he wants banana cream he asks for lemon meringue. It's friendly. You get to know that kind of thing about the regulars. It doesn't cost you anything.

"How I loved driving those roads. When Robert picked me up I would always keep the windows rolled up for the first little while. Even on a warm night like this. The car always smelled of leather. He re-did those seats three times before he got them the way he wanted. Sure, I know what his friends said about why he did the inside of the car first, but I never listened to that kind of talk. Neither did he. It did say something about him though. Even now I can see that it says something. He started from the inside and worked out. That car must have been dabbed up with primer for three years after I met him, but he didn't care. It had to be right for him on the inside before he worried about the outside and what other people saw. He didn't care about what people said. And I believe that is best. Always take care of the inside first, and let people say what they want." Jennifer's voice stops. Perhaps she is pondering the wisdom of what she has said. She has the yellow lantern. Her hand is up to her hair, touching it, smoothing it, and touching it again like a moth circling a light.

"What is it they used to say?" My grandmother has taken up the story once more. Her light is the green lantern that has faded almost to grey. It is quiet, unobtrusive light, almost like shadow. "Oh yes, I remember it now. It was a kind of poem: Can day be night? Can left be right? Can young be old? Can hot be cold? Is his love both warm and real? Is it ice or flame you feel? Then they would take an ice cube and touch it to the back of your neck. It was at Bunny Parker's. She always had some game like that. Or fortune-telling or palm-reading. She clipped that game from the Chicago newspaper her father took. Whatever it was she always said it was the latest

thing. Of course, after all that talk, you were bound to think it was a flame. But I held on. I said ice even though it felt like flame. That's how I was back then. She was so let down. She told all the others, 'Only Ruby's love is true.' Her family went back to North Dakota.... Now, hot and cold. What was I thinking? Hot and cold. They get mixed up. Like on those really hot days when it rains just a few big drops and it is almost like they are burning when they hit your back. It rained like that the day John died. Yes that was it. That is what I was thinking. It was hot that day too...."

Like moths around a light or Jennifer's hands around her hair, my grandmother's thoughts have been circling. Now they have landed upon the day that her youngest son, John, died. Possibly because he hears that her voice is settling and about to land, Grandfather wheels from the verandah railing. "Damn." He walks abruptly, too abruptly, down the length of the verandah. He moves impatiently, as if to make Grandmother's thoughts rise up and fly away again. He clatters down the steps and stops halfway down the sidewalk. "Ruby. Ruby, stop your mumbling and listen. Is it the Peacock boy?" There is a double explosion of sound as the car goes over the railroad tracks southeast of town. "It's the Arnson boy for sure. If that boy used half the grease on his car that he uses on his hair they'd both get a lot further. Ha!" His laugh is a single syllable as explosive as the rattle from the car. He does it again, "Ha!"

The Origin of the Grapefruit Tree

My grandfather had a grapefruit tree that would not bloom. Every year he waited for it to bloom and bear fruit, and every year he was disappointed. Not one blossom appeared upon its branches until the spring he died, and then the tree bloomed and bore fruit all in one day, affirming in a cruel and ironic way that dreams sometimes do come true.

I have been thinking about his grapefruit tree. Perhaps I feel obliged to explain away its late and ironic productivity for the same reason he provided a yearly excuse for its barrenness. On the other hand, the grapefruit tree might be haunting me simply because there is a good story hidden among its branches. The right ingredients are present: a moral, a picturesque grandfather, a naïve young boy, a small town and a long hot summer for the plot to unfold.

And there is a marvellous first sentence: My grandfather had a grapefruit tree that would not bloom. Such a sentence might begin a story of failed dreams. It also suggests both the fairytale and the folktale; trees that bear fruit perpetually and trees that are cursed and barren are often found in both genres (now that I think of it, there is even a slight biblical allusion). A story grows so naturally from a good first sentence that I could almost finish this one in the space of a paragraph:

> The tree grew, spiky and unrepentant, at the end of the verandah of the house he built in the town of Union. He had moved to Union at the age of 41, leaving his homestead to his eldest son. He came to town dreaming of civilization; he built his house, established the first hardware store, planted his orchard and settled back to become a founding citizen of a growing community. But though he had reached three score and ten, Union never grew, and the grapefruit tree never bore fruit. I was young and inno-

cent, and in that early summer of my life I did not understand about broken dreams.

There you have it: an old man's disillusion and a young boy's dream are both recalled by an older and wiser narrator. Most readers could fill in the remaining details, and I can think of many stories that are written along similar lines. The Old Man, the Young Boy, the Hot Summer, and so on, provide fertile if somewhat sentimental ground for storytellers. My story, however, is going to require much more than one paragraph. Indeed, it was that summer more than two decades ago that forever removed from me the possibility of telling the kind of sentimental tale that I have just outlined. Fortunately, the first sentence can remain.

My grandfather had a grapefruit tree that would not bloom. At least, he claimed it was a grapefruit tree, and for all I know he was right. It certainly resembled no tree I had ever seen before or have ever seen since. In fact, it only vaguely resembled a tree.

I picture the tree in a kind of tableau of the seasons. In the spring, before its leaves came out, it reminded me of a medieval mace, one of those lethal looking pincushions-on-a-stick that can be seen beside the suit of armour in even the most impoverished of civic museums. In the summer, filled in with leaves, it became the parody of a real tree; like a child's drawing, its pole-like brown trunk would be topped by a cumulus cloud of green leaves. In the fall, its perverse rib-cage once again apparent but its basic symmetry still marred by the broken twigs and dead leaves caught in its branches, it was a giant magpie's nest.

Oddly enough, it was its winter appearance that most strongly supported my grandfather's claim that it was a grapefruit tree; it is the winter image that I now remember best. Cleaned to its essentials by the wind, its quills poking out through the dusting of snow that clung to its boll, the tree achieved an unnatural barrenness. Standing in three feet of snow, it was a skeletal silhouette of a beach umbrella, its fabric torn off and its spines blown inside out, abandoned on some cold and bitter beach. Then, when the sun set early in the middle of winter, seen through the frosted front-room window, only a grapefruit tree—planted in a country where the winters are six months long—only a grapefruit tree could look so desolate in the falling evening.

Now, regardless of how convincing the tree's winter appearance might have been or how insistent my grandfather was about its identity, I find myself uncertain about whether or not it was a grapefruit tree. For that matter, I am not even sure it could properly be called my grandfather's tree because my grandmother and my grandfather each had different versions of the tree's origin.

I heard my grandfather's story both first and last; he narrated and embellished his version of the origin myth every year until the spring he died. The first time I must have been somewhere between four and six years old. We were standing on the verandah in surprisingly warm Easter sunshine. A fly, awakened by the warmth, buzzed drunkenly on the warm cement. My sister, mother and father, as well as various aunts, uncles and cousins were inside getting ready to go to Uncle Edwin's farm for Easter dinner, and the fuss had created a bond between Grandfather and me something like that shared by bachelors at a wedding reception. By a series of leading questions he had manoeuvred me into expressing doubt about the existence of a grapefruit tree in such a northern latitude. In later years I recognized this as one of his tactics when faced with a new audience, but then I believed I was hearing an exclusive or at least spontaneous narration.

That first version relied heavily upon Jack and the Beanstock. Grandfather gave himself the starring role. It was the spring of 1923. A boxcar containing a shipment of grapefruit had been mistakenly shunted north from a location he always referred to as "some damn Yankee paradise where cold is just a state of mind." After an amazing journey that featured endless snow-covered plains, periodic sojourns at various railroad sidings and incredible bureaucratic foul-ups by the CPR, the boxcar had arrived at Union's railway station. The grapefruit were still largely unspoiled because of the cold weather, making them, he said, the first example of refrigerated transport of produce.

He was waiting at the station that day to accept delivery of a horsehair sofa, although in later versions it became a radio, a refrigerator or whatever else happened to suit his purpose. The boxcar was opened and he was so amazed at the appearance of citrus in such a northern latitude (he always referred to grapefruit as citrus, thus managing to give it the properties of an essence rather than a fruit) that he traded his sofa straight across for six cases of the fruit. He described my grandmother's disgust and the town's derision as he and my grandmother were forced to eat grapefruit after grapefruit in the days that followed. When the grapefruit days were finally over, he planted one of the seeds.

Then, standing in the rare grace of Easter sunshine, before a totally convinced audience of one, he became strangely vehement. "And if you don't believe me, then by gawd you go over there and touch her because there she is right there." He took me by the shoulder. His grip was strong and yet, in the way old people have, querulous, as if he were trying to lead me and lean on me at the same time. We made our way down to the end of the verandah. When we stepped into the shadow of the tree, the change in light momentarily blinded me. He made me reach out and touch the trunk; it was smooth, cool, and in a curious way, receding before my grasp.

It was then he put the question, "Well, is she real?" It seemed he was shouting it in my ear and squeezing my shoulder even harder as he did so. I carefully mumbled my reply three times before I was sure that my response was correct. "Sing it out," he kept repeating, and I finally sang it out, "Yes Grandfather, she's real." He let go of my shoulder and ended it the way he was to end it for the next seven years. "Sooner or later, and maybe this year, she's going to bloom and bear fruit. Then by gawd, they'll have something to stare at. Then, by gawd, how they'll sit up and shout."

I was not to see such vehemence again until years later in his final rendition of the story, when it did no good at all. It was entirely unnecessary on that first day. I believed him completely, and the tree, which had been totally anonymous, became an object of special interest to me. Of course, in the years that followed, I believed the story less and less, but I enjoyed it more and more. As the details he added became more outlandish the whole story became more real. In my mind's eye I can still see picture after picture from his final version. I can see all the townspeople assembled in a drab, mumbling group around the boxcar making inane suggestions about the nature of the fluid that dripped out of the bottom and into the flinty gravel between the railroad ties. And there is the deep blue of the boxcar itself, startling in front of the grey springtime sky. I can smell the heady, half-astringent, half-decayed odour that assailed their nostrils when he courageously stepped forward and rolled the big doors back. Best of all, and with no effort whatsoever, I can see the beautifully round, brilliantly yellow grapefruit avalanching out of the car and onto the station's weathered boardwalk, rolling and bounding and tumbling in an endless sunbright wave toward the amazed, slack-jawed townspeople.

Although I only heard my grandmother's version of the origin of the grapefruit tree once, her story is equally vivid in my memory. I was nine years old. My mother, father, grandmother and I were driving back from Thanksgiving dinner at the farm. Grandfather was driving home in his truck with my sister and a cousin. Uncle Edwin's farm was the place that my grandparents had homesteaded, and because my grandmother felt she had spent the best years of her life there, she was always pensive when returning to Union. Indeed, with the long day and the big meal, we were all quiet.

As was often the case, I was not really listening to what she had to say. Now I sometimes regret that I did not because she actually had a great number of interesting stories. Unfortunately, she delivered them in long, pause-filled monologues that led me to consider them not as authentic histories but more as "The time that Grandmother fed the hungry Indian when there was no-one home, which takes 45 minutes to tell," or "The journey in the Red River Cart from the railroad to the homestead, which takes up to two hours to tell."

On those trips back to Union, however, she was more inclined to simply recite the geneologies of the farmhouses that we passed. A mere glimpse of a yard light behind a cara-gana windbreak would set off the dry, rambling voice. "A young couple in the Baker Place now...Baker's son-in-law... What was his name?...married Ella Baker in '33...It was the same day as Edna and Roy got married and it caused bad feeling. Some folks didn't know which to go to...Jones, Lloyd Jones...they say he married Ella for Old Tom Baker's farm...you know he died six years ago, just two years after Ella...and I said I guess that goes to show he just wasn't in it for the farm after all...young couple have it now...no rela-tion to the Bakers. No relation to Lloyd Jones...just up and bought it...five years ago...don't do their business in Union...just strangers really, but then they've only been here five years..." With the dashboard casting its gentle green light over the front seat and the insects making their swift, hypnotic arcs into the headlights, the distinction between waking and sleeping would become blurred. Her dry, droning voice blended with the static crackle of the gravel underneath the wheels of the car; I cannot be sure if it was my grandmother or the night who told the story on that journey back to Union. It was her mention of the grapefruit tree that kept me from finally going to sleep. I did not sit up and take notice. Instead it was more as if the well into which her voice was dropping suddenly became deeper and more still.

Once again it was 1923, and once again my grandfather had the starring role. He had been hiccupping for two nights and three days. The local doctor and the man he had called in to consult were both completely baffled. For the first day and a half he lay in relative seclusion. The townspeople had known about the hiccups, but it had not become a *cause célèbre* until the second day around noon. Almost simultaneously, everyone decided that Grandfather's condition was truly serious and not just mildly amusing. In true and much fabled smalltown fashion they began to tender their advice. It began as a trickle, but by late afternoon it turned into a flood.

Sitting in the front seat of the car I ceased to notice the insects, the road or the willows that could be seen whipping by either side of the corridor the headlights made. Instead I was watching as an incredible assortment of people paraded up the street, fumbled with the front gate, left curls of rich spring mud on the boot scraper and mounted the stairs to my grandparents' front door.

Like suitors for the hand of the princess in all of the fairytales I had ever read, they spoke their magic words to Grandmother and then waited on the verandah, patiently viewing the growing crowd in the street and hoping that their incantation would be the one to break the spell. Sooner or later my grandmother would come back down and speak to them from the door. They would trudge down the stairs, the insistent hiccupping from the upstairs window echoing their defeat.

At first the cures they suggested were commonplace. He was forced to look at himself in a mirror while he hiccupped; he was told to drink water from the wrong side of the glass; he was obliged to consume a tablespoon full of sugar. Then the variations started. During the morning of the third day he had to drink vinegar, apple cider, cold milk, warm milk, buttermilk and tea made from dandelions and rainwater, all from the wrong side of the glass. He downed tablespoons full of coffee grounds, breadcrumbs, tealeaves and even sawdust. Cold packs were placed on his feet and forehead; warm packs were placed on his forehead and feet. He held his breath. He was instructed to avoid breathing. But no matter how devious the cures became, none of them worked.

By the afternoon of the third day almost the entire town had gathered in the street in front of the house, and as each disappointed petitioner had walked disconsolately back down the stairs, the crowd gained another committed participant. At any other time such a unified expression of concern would have been accepted by Grandfather as a just and long overdue acknowledgement of his position as a founding citizen of Sortie County, something that Union consistently denied him in the yearly election of town officers. It became apparent, however, that they were assembled not out of respect but out of a lurid curiosity.

I can picture him on the afternoon of that third day sitting up in his bed, weak from hiccupping, weak from lack of food and most of all weak from the cures that he had survived. His glossy, nut-brown, bald head had become wan and pale, achieving the slightly greenish tinge usually found only on the last grapefruit on the produce stand at the supermarket. Outside, the crowd could be heard growing more restive by the moment, but when Mr. Swartz, the town butcher, approached the house with his ladder and gunny sack the crowd hushed. Children stopped racing about. Lounging men straightened. Women stopped chatting. Even the horses, which had been tied to the fence, noticed the hush and looked up expectantly. Placing the ladder quietly against the window-sill and carefully taking a partially decomposed cow's head from the gunny sack, he silently began to mount the ladder.

Mr. Swartz had been the only German-Canadian in Union during the war and for the first few years following it. Knowing that anything he said during that time could and would be used against him, he had become a silent man. That day it was almost as if my grandfather's rebelling diaphragm had struck a note of sympathy in Mr. Swartz. As he raised the decomposed cow's head over the sill of the window he loosed a piercing battle cry. The force of his scream drove him backwards off the ladder, and the decomposed cow's head made a giant, pinwheeling arc toward the crowd below; its descent served as a signal for the beginning of repeated attempts to frighten the hiccups from my grandfather. The one or two boys who had managed to save firecrackers from the previous July set them off beneath Grandfather's window. Three of the town's six veterans, taking their cue from the firecrackers, brought out souvenir rifles and fired them off in unison. Because cleaning cotton had been left in the barrel of one of the rifles, the effect was impressive. The sound of the exploding rifle and the subsequent scream of pain and surprise from Wesley Stoller was sincere enough to make Grandfather rise up on one elbow and ask if anyone was hurt. Discovering that Mr. Stoller had been holding the weapon at arm's length and had only received a mildly lacerated hand, he lay back again, disappointed and still hiccupping. Arnold Peacock, the man who had helped Grandfather build his house, stood beneath the window and loudly remarked that a year-old house should not have a crack in the foundation that you could put a broom handle into. Reginald Bateman, the volunteer Fire Marshall, rang the Baptist Church bell while his four sons shouted at the top of their voices that the hardware store was on fire. Mrs. Rose stood beneath the window and remarked to Ella Peacock that she had seen my grandmother and Ella's brother, Arnold, walking hand in hand down by the river.

But regardless of how many subterfuges were attempted, my grandfather's hiccups proved as impervious to shock and fear as they had been to sawdust and vinegar. The only real effect of that afternoon's outburst was upon John MacLenan, the one man in Union who had actually seen front-line duty in the war and had returned home with shell shock. He suffered a relapse, and taking cover in the unfinished basement of the United Church was not discovered until 24 hours later.

As we neared Union that night, adventure after adventure appeared before my eyes. Men who had been dead before I was born were resurrected and set upon the roof with hammers to pound the shingles above my grandfather's head. Women whom I had seen in Mr. Swartz's butcher shop, standing awkward and faded before the glass counter trying to decide between beef and pork for the Sunday roast, were transformed into lithe, just-budding beauties who moved through the crowd glancing appraisingly at the antics of husbands-to-be. Other men whom I knew as quiet figures who smelled of tobacco and breathed noisily through their noses were described swinging on the fence and dangling by their legs from tree branches. The whole town seemed to frolic up and down the street, performing antic after antic until it seemed they had forgotten why they had come; until it seemed that the afternoon sunlight would slant down from the same angle for ever and ever so that a traveller, even years later, could happen upon their celebration.

Indeed, but for Mrs. Roget perhaps it would have gone on forever. Mrs. Roget was a quasi-professional herb doctor, faith healer, witch and distiller who lived in the River Hills. Word had finally filtered out to her about my grandfather's condition, and she journeyed to town to offer her assistance. Undoubtedly relying on her quasi-professional, hypnotic glance, she walked straight into the house past my grandmother. Remarking she would be glad to have tea when she came back downstairs, she went up to Grandfather's room. My grandmother was unutterably weary by this time, and she obediently went to the kitchen to make tea. It was not until about five minutes later that she went up to see how the cure was progressing. Grandfather was sitting up in bed with a red kerchief around his head from which a feather protruded Indian style from the back. Mrs. Roget was conducting the ritual with another feather at the foot of the bed. In Grandfather's left hand was a still-warm hardboiled egg. In his right hand was an apple. The family Bible was propped up on his knees and he was reading aloud from it. His diaphragm was making the recitation blasphemous. He had just reached "And the evening and the morning were the third day" when Grandmother walked in. Quietly but efficiently she removed his feather, apple and egg. With equal efficiency she removed Mrs. Roget. Having begun, she did not stop. Escorting Mrs. Roget right down the walk, she had a few quiet and clear words with three or four of her neighbours.

The townspeople straggled home, and the town became silent like a fairground after a fair. The street was cluttered with paper from packed lunches, an occasional screendoor slapped shut and John MacLenan's wife periodically called out for her husband to come home for supper as if he were a ten-year-old late from baseball instead of a veteran quaking in the foundation of the United Church. The timeless peace of early evening descended, and the only sounds left to recall the afternoon's pandemonium were the buzzing of a few flies over the manure where the horses had been tied and the hic that came from the upstairs window with calm, cricket-like regularity.

Into this peace came the last suitor. As in all the fairytales I had ever read, he was not what one would expect of a hero. Meek and mild (and so he was even when I knew him years later), Mr. Elliot made the long walk from Elliot's General Merchandise to my grandparents' house. In his hand was a brown paper bag. In the brown paper bag was a grapefruit.

"Now Ruby, I know you're upset, but this ain't a cure. I just thought maybe you could give him the juice. Kind of a treat like. You don't see these in this part of the country every day. Maybe it'll build him up." My grandmother let him in and the potion was prepared.

Grandfather took the juice and judiciously began to drink it between hiccups, grateful, no doubt, that he could drink it from the right side of the glass and that it was not vinegar. Suddenly be began to gasp and thrash and heave himself about on the bed. Grandmother and Mr. Elliot watched in amazement, fearful that he had reached some kind of hiccup crisis and was expiring. Suddenly Mr. Elliot realized what was happening: "He's choking, Ruby, he's choking." Grandmother grabbed a volume of the encyclopedia that was kept beside the bed for Grandfather's nightly reading, and just as he was changing from a wan yellow to blue, she struck him on the back.

A grapefruit seed flew out of his mouth. After all of the gasping and the thrashing about, after all of the shouting and shooting and pandemonium of the afternoon, and indeed, after the three days and two nights of ceaseless and insistent hiccupping, the seed rested upon the bedclothes like a pearl of stillness.

All three of them were stunned into sudden immobility by the silence. The afternoon sun beamed in through the windows, making sharp shadows and dramatic highlights; the folds of the bedclothes looked sculpted. Grandfather was holding up the empty glass, and it caught the sun brightly as he stared first at the glass and then down at the bedclothes where the seed still lay. My grandmother's hand was up to her cheek in a kind of silent-movie gesture of dismay. Mr. Elliot leaned forward with great intensity, the expression of concern on his face becoming imperceptibly closer to an expression of joy as the silence continued to grow.

The silence grew and grew until it was as bright and certain as the sunlight. It became apparent that the words to break such a silence had to be portentous. They had to reanimate an historic moment, and so they had to be historic themselves, or perhaps all three people would have remained forever frozen. It was, of course, my grandfather who spoke. Tentatively, still worried that unasked for punctuation would mar the sentence, and with the mortal tones of a man who had come to the bank of the river and had been reaching into his back pocket to pay the ferryman, he said: "Plant that seed, girl. It's a miracle fruit. Plant the seed."

It was not until years later that I realized why I was able to picture that final scene of my grandmother's story so vividly. It was long after my grandfather's death, when I was helping Grandmother move her belongings out of the house that I realized that the picture that hung above their bed bore a striking resemblance to the picture I had in my mind of the termination of Grandfather's hiccups. It was a calendar reproduction of David's "Socrates Drinking Hemlock," one of the old standards of the French Neo-classical school.

Leaving aside the irony of comparing Socrates and my grandfather, the fact remains that my grandmother did plant the grapefruit seed. Whether or not it actually grew into the tree at the end of the verandah, she was not willing to decide. "A tree is just a tree" was her final comment as we walked toward the house that night. Nevertheless, by telling her story she had planted another kind of seed. Instead of debunking my grandfather's claims, she made me more interested in the whole question. What might have become just another tree was touched by controversy. It grew in my thoughts.

Of course the tree itself was indifferent to its origin. In fact, the winter image of the grapefruit tree that I carry with me now goes so far beyond indifference that it almost issues a challenge. During that last summer, however, the tree did not have to issue any challenge to capture my attention. I badly needed to believe in something, and through a series of circumstances, it became the focus of that need. Indeed, sometimes I think I am still standing in its shadows.

I spent the summer of my twelfth year in Union because

of a whim of my parents. They first met when my father passed through Union in the summer of 1935 showing moving pictures from the back of a flatbed truck. He had a portable screen, projector and sound system, and he made a circuit of about 300 miles. He would drive into town, set up in any hall or auditorium that was available and charge the townspeople a dime to see Clark Gable, Charlie Chaplin, Greta Garbo, Louise Brooks and any number of other, lesser lights. My mother eloped with him, and they continued riding the circuit for the rest of that summer. He ran the projector, and she took the tickets. They were both capable of becoming highly nostalgic about that time of their lives, and when I was twelve, my father decided it would be good to try it again, further north. It was going to be just like a second honeymoon, but he was going to make his own film of the venture. Having participated in a number of documentaries, he felt it was time for his masterwork. As it turned out, they were later to recall the summer as just another of his many attempts to escape industrial public relations. My sister was to spend the summer with the family of her best friend who had moved to Montreal that spring. I was to spend the summer with my grandparents.

Even at the age of twelve, I believe I understood my parents' nostalgia; I think I felt somewhat the same way about the town of Union. In fact, regardless of the intervening years (and the events of that summer), I can still recall what Union meant to me for the first eleven years of my life.

Until that summer my only contact with Union had been on the dates of the calendar that made the long drive possible: Christmas, Easter, Victoria Day and Thanksgiving Day were, by tradition, spent in Union. They were the festival days, and they were responsible for my attitude to the town and my grandparents' house. Now, in retrospect, they seem to be very innocent days.

The first memory that comes to me is of the bank of windows in a succession of schoolrooms turned into stained-

25

glass by taping coloured pictures to the panes. When a holiday approached we would be given mimeographed outlines of Easter eggs and rabbits, or Christmas trees and reindeer, or whatever icon best represented the coming event. Liberally supplied with wax crayons, we would fill the last, dozing hour of the day with colour while the teacher nodded and kept a passive eye on that one child each year who, because he was not being given proper scope for his frustrated creativity, or because certain crayons looked edible, would horrify the more fastidious among us by grimacing with red or purple stained teeth. Then, in the intervening days before the holiday, the pictures would colour the sunlight, making it seem as if the house lights had been dimmed in anticipation of the approaching festivity.

The journey to Union never failed to live up to the expectations generated in the preceding days. We would leave in the evening, and at some point while we were still on paved highway, passing motels, gas stations, overpasses and underpasses, I would go to sleep. When I awakened everything would be changed. Now, if I wished, I could calculate the distance that we covered in miles or the time that I slept in hours, but such numbers would be meaningless.

I would awaken with the gentle swaying motion of a car on a gravelled road. The darkness would be perfect. It was not simply a matter of absence of light; there was the corridor the headlights made and the glow from the dashboard that silhouetted my mother, father and sister in the front seat. Nor was it simply a matter of the overwhelming change from the straight well-lit highway, loud with headlights and tail-lights and signs. Instead the darkness was perfect because it was imaginary; it was the kind of darkness I can remember envisioning from the one or two radio plays I heard at those times when a television was not available. The reason for this radio darkness was simply that I knew we were driving through the deep and mysterious forest the citizens of Union called the River Hills. By a freak circum-

26

stance, the town of Union had been denied a wrong side of the tracks; the entire town was on the south side. Nor did they have an East side, a West side or a seamy waterfront. Denied all of the classic "bad" parts of town, they heaped all of their unused drama on the River Hills, the gullies and breaks of the Sortie River.

The River Hills became the place where cars were tumbled off embankments by the infamous and apparently numberless sons of Mr. Hueffer who were all destined, I was told, for a bad end. Even otherwise upstanding young men could go astray in the River Hills, and young girls were continually losing their reputations by simple proximity to the Hills' baleful influence. On some nights mysterious bonfires could be seen winking there in the trees across the river. Mrs. Roget lived in them, and there was even a legend of a resident Wildman that had considerable currency among those under ten years of age.

It was in these very same hills that I would awaken, usually to hear strange and ominous utterances from my parents and sister. They would be saying things like "How I wish they would straighten up this God-forsaken road," or "What was that up ahead?" or even "These hills seem to grow steeper every year."

By sitting up very quietly and saying nothing I would achieve a practical invisibility, and that was the way I preferred to approach Union: silent and invisible, out of the dark of night and the even darker shadows of the River Hills.

So it was as the invisible man from the enchanted forest—a potent and sinister amalgam that I was quite comfortable with—that I would catch my first glimpse of Union. I would see the lights dancing in the forest, appearing and disappearing as we wound around and over the River Hills. Sometimes they seemed close and sometimes they seemed farther away, but as lights dancing in the forest are supposed to do, they seemed to entice us deeper and deeper

27

into the trees. And like any lights glimpsed intermittently through trees, the lights of Union gave the impression of a cleared and secure place where all the tangles of the forest could be left behind.

When we arrived in Union, I would have to become a normal, small boy once again, at least momentarily. My grandparents would be standing side by side on the verandah with the porch light shining behind them like some advertisement for a homecoming. Grandmother, completely unaware of who she was dealing with, would give me a hug and a kiss and make customary exclamations about how I had grown. In fact I kept careful track of my size and occasionally I would not have grown even a quarter-inch, but this did not seem to matter to her. My grandfather, however, because he sensed he was in the presence of some secret force, or simply because of a pathological inability to engage in conventional social acts, would shake my hand and ask me how the wife and kids were doing or some other equally out of context banality. I would dutifully smile through it all, meanwhile checking from the corner of my eye to see if the grapefruit tree was blooming, or depending on the time of year, simply to ascertain that it had not been cut down because of my grandmother's fears for the foundation. Then, when everyone began to rush about unpacking the car and setting the tea, I could become invisible once again.

In an unlikely frame of mind, which I recall as a cross between that of a sorcerer's apprentice trespassing on the inner sanctum, and that of a smug merchant surveying a well-stocked storeroom, I would make an inventory of the house. I would begin with the dining-room. It was redolent with lemon oil, and polished and burnished so thoroughly that even the one beam of light that came in from the hall would leap from the sideboard, rebound off the table and remain echoing in the gleaming porcelain in the china cabinet, suffusing the whole room with a mahogany glow. It was a solemn and dignified space, and I would walk around the

28

perimeter of the dining-room table with great care, one hand resting upon its surface to sample its smoothness. At the far end of the sideboard there was a nut bowl carved from wood with a pedestal at its centre from which a silver nut-cracker surrounded by silver nut-picks protruded like a crown. I would pause, reach up to see if there were still nuts in the bowl, and feeling tentatively around for the unmistakeably smooth contours of a walnut, I would speculate whether these nuts were the same ones that had been in the bowl during my last visit, or even the visit before that. Only once had I seen someone offend the solemnity of the room by actually cracking a nut and eating it. He was rewarded for his barbaric disregard of the room's ambience by a swift change in complexion and a hurried trip outside. With this memory in mind I would examine the walnut in my hand, and delighted by its warmth and dull shine, I would carefully hold it up to my nose. The faint odour of lemon oil would re-establish my belief that for some reason my grandmother had polished the nuts as well as the sideboard.

After placing the walnut carefully back in the bowl, I would move down to the silver dish at the other end of the sideboard. It was filled with dusty white peppermints. I would take one and hold it in my mouth for the rest of my journey around the house, always resolving to note the exact moment when it disappeared into nothingness. I always failed. I would become aware of a taste in the back of my throat tantalizingly similar to that faint taste produced by smelling mothballs. I would realize that, once again, I had failed to note that split second when the peppermint disappeared, and at the same time, begin to argue myself out of the notion that my grandmother had substituted mothballs for mints.

The kitchen was a bastion of orderly rows of cups, cannisters and framed Norman Rockwell prints. After the dimness of the dining-room, the bright light bouncing off the ceramic tiles of the floor and walls made it seem like I was standing inside a flame. But on the window-ledge, between a green glass flower vase and a daisy pressed between two panes of glass, stood a small bronze donkey. Actually to call the figure a donkey is a mistake; it was, as my grandmother so often said, a jackass. It stood with its head thrown back in a grotesque fashion, and its mouth open as if to bray. It was green and piebald with age except for the tips of its upper and lower teeth where its use as a bottle opener had kept the original bronze glow shining. This gleam just at the tips of its teeth gave the jackass a particularly lewd and gaudy expression. Even now when someone offers me any sort of alcohol I can remember my grandmother's admonition whenever she caught me staring in fascination at the ugly figurine. "He is a jackass, Jonathan. Not a donkey. Not a mule. But a jackass. I will tell you why. He has been used to open too many bottles of beer, Jonathan, and you should remember that if you are ever tempted by alcohol." And if my grandfather happened to be sitting in his chair in the kitchen, he would invariably remark: "Ruby, you've told that story so many times it's a wonder he doesn't go to sleep." To make his point, he would throw his head back and yawn ostentatiously; his gold fillings would glint in a way that was frighteningly reminiscent of the jackass.

After visiting the jackass I would make my way into the front room. There, on a table by the front window, was an equally disturbing and fascinating object. It was a glass globe containing four red roses. Their mystery lay in the fact that I could never decide if they were real roses contained in some sort of clear fluid or if they were in fact porcelain roses. I would begin with the notion that real roses could not be so perfect and unflawed. They would have to have one petal torn away or a slight discolouration or some other similar variation if they were real, and so I reasoned they must be porcelain. But stepping closer, I would realize that no-one could make such perfect porcelain roses; each was a slightly different shade of red, and just slightly different in shape. I would conclude that they must be real. But then stepping closer again I would be unable to believe that four such roses had ever grown in a garden.

And as I stepped closer and closer the roses would begin to shift back and forth between reality and artifice so quickly they would begin to shimmer like a heatwave. By the time I reached the table, I would believe that I was very close to the secret. My hands on the table, I would bend down to stare straight into the globe for the final decision. My sense of impending revelation would disappear, and I would find myself staring at the porch light, the grapefruit tree and the houses of Union, all reflected upside down and in miniature in the glass globe. The diffraction of the globe made the branches of the tree balloon out so that they seemed to cover the entire town like a kind of web.

Now, the vision of the grapefruit tree superimposed over the town seems ominous, but then it only served to remind me of the many possibilities awaiting me on the next day, and I would contentedly leave the roses unsolved and move into the front hall for the final two stops on my itinerary.

The first was a picture that I referred to as the Lonely Elk. The Lonely Elk hung in perpetual shadow behind the dining-room door that opened into the front hall. I would step completely behind the door to view him. The picture had been painted by my Uncle John many years before. He had died two years afterwards, but my grandmother had told me about him and the painting many times. It had been done with leftover housepaints and an old piece of board, and as my grandmother had said, it made you wonder what he might have done with real brushes and canvas and paint. Indeed, she felt if he had lived he would have been a great artist. The surprising thing is that in a puzzling way she was right about the picture.

The scene portrayed was typical enough, an elk was standing by a mountain river at dusk; the whole thing could have been copied from a calendar. Furthermore, the elk was out of perspective. If you looked objectively the elk would have had to have been somewhere between fifteen and twenty feet high with an antler spread like the crown of an oak tree. But regardless of these discrepancies the picture was fascinating because Uncle John—who my grandmother said had never seen an elk in all his short life—had actually caught some kind of essence.

The elk was looking across the river toward the mountains on the other side. The sun had just set behind them; the far side of the river was all in shadow. The river reflected the light in the sky so that the elk was in silhouette against the water. His head was up and he seemed to be peering over the river. There was a quality of listening about his posture as if he had heard something there and was trying to ascertain what it was. I have never seen an elk outside the zoo, but I am as sure today as I was then that the picture showed how they must look at such times. I think I called it the Lonely Elk because Uncle John had caught the nature of something very like loneliness or at least loneliness as I understood it as a child. He had caught the vacancy of apprehension that can overtake you when you wake from a vivid dream and are not sure where you are; or the sudden mind-clearing surprise when you step out of a theatre in the evening after you entered it in the daylight, and the obvious purpose in the bright lights and the passersby can make you feel lost for a moment.

Perhaps I am overestimating the picture's achievement. It could be that I stared so intently, trying to see what the elk was trying to see, that when I stepped back out from behind the door into the hallway the sudden change in light and space gave the picture more effect than it would have had otherwise. I also recall that when I was six years old my grandfather caught me gazing at it and remarked, casually, "I guess that old elk is curious about what those three fellas are doing across the river." I had to get a kitchen chair to stand on to look at the picture more closely before I realized that he was teasing me.

The second article in the front hall was an old treadle sewing-machine that sat by the bathroom door. My grandmother kept it, she said, in case she might want to do some sewing some time when the power was out, but it was more likely retained out of nostalgia. In any event, with the machine folded down in its cabinet it served well as a hall table. It collected all of the usual articles a hall table collects, but if it had not been for its one regular tenant, a globe of the world, it would not have been mysterious at all. As it was, the combination of the treadle machine and the globe allowed me to perform a ritual which was, as I remember it now, close to the heart and soul of the house. The process was simple. The treadle of such a machine is balanced so that once you begin, it is almost as if the machine takes a life of its own and moves your foot rather than the other way around. While treadling it, I would lean up against the table and begin to spin the globe. The combination of treadling and spinning must have been almost hypnotic. With my finger resting lightly on its faintly uneven surface, I would first imagine I was feeling the earth's surface, and then after a short while, I could literally see it turning beneath me, first just fields and fences and gravel roads, and then higher and faster for mountains and rivers and oceans and deserts, and finally just a whirling, humming blur that had all of the house and Union and the journey over the River Hills somehow blended into a single sensation; I thought of it to myself as Treadling the World.

Of course, no matter how long I stood there treadling the world, the tea would finally be brewed, and I would be called to the kitchen. My invisibility would fade. But the mystery of the house never faded. There was always some of it left for the next day or for that matter, the next visit. And so it continued until my final summer when more than ever before I needed the mystery to be substantial. Even now, when I know that the secret and mysterious delights of

33

Union were only the product of imagination and not tangible at all, I still have a lingering wish to believe. Before I recount the events that led up to my final visit, I am inclined to let my younger self go to bed once more in a world where the joys and mysteries were real and only the fears were circumscribed.

I would change to my nightgown in the bathroom, and then after a formal series of "Goodnights," I would dash down the stairs, across the rough, hand-poured concrete of the unfinished portion of the basement and into the safety of the bedroom. Once safe, I would look back out; there was the root cellar with its nightmare growth of potato sprouts reaching vainly for the light; there was the coal cellar where unwary boys were buried by the careless coalman; and there was the frost heave, silent, but powerful and growing over by the stairs. But then I would be safe in bed, the dusty sachet smell of the sheets and the moist earth smell of the basement combining so that the scent of fresh lilacs pervaded the room. And all night long the dead, black canes of last year's raspberries would tapdance against the window, and the frost heave would silently meditate upon new sources of strength from the earth's core, and the cracked remnant of linoleum outside the bedroom door would curl and uncurl in frustration at having missed me once again. I would be protected, sleeping a deep, deep, deep sleep, and dreaming enchanted dreams.

The Mermaid and the Mystery of Life

Protection is what I wanted from the town of Union that summer. Earlier in the city, I encountered what my grandfather called the mystery of life. That spring it seemed that

34

every child in the neighbourhood arrived before the Mystery of Life at the same time. In games of hide-and-seek Dianne Webster and Laddie Deptford, thirteen and fifteen respectively, would hide and not be found all evening until one of us would inadvertently stumble across them in such romantic places as under the tarp of Jenson's motorboat or in the Walden's half finished garage behind the pile of lumber. I remember Dianne and Laddie in particular because I was an expert at hide-and-seek, and I had a curious respect for whatever force drove them to discover locations that were previously known only to me.

It was not only members of the older set who were infected. On rainy days, from garages or under porches, children who were even three or four years younger than myself could be heard talking in hushed and solemn voices about the atrocities committed upon women by Nazis, Indians and members of the Purple Gang, a mythical group of youths who were supposed to have congregated in the city centre some few years before. There were muttered conversations about where babies came from, classic performances of Doctor and Nurse, and many complex contractual negotiations of the "I'll show you if you'll show me" variety in and around the abandoned shack that served as shelter for skaters in the winter-time. I was too young for the delights of kissing behind piles of lumber, but I was too old to play doctor. I could only observe the goings on, and it began to seem not so much like a series of specific instances as it was a general air in the neighbourhood. It was almost like a scent. Seasons did seem to have scents in those days: cut grass, burning leaves, hot dust on the radiators, and wet wood and road tar. That spring it was once again wet wood and road tar, but there was also something else; young boys looked more closely at discarded, rain-smeared magazines in hopes they would see one of Those Magazines, and young girls were suddenly stretching their voices in a high, nervous parody of knowing laughter if a neighbourhood girl was seen going out with a boy.

Whatever that scent was, it was most noticeable and yet most undefined at the playground. The Capitol Hill Tots to Teens Playground had always been of particular interest to me because it was there that I first learned the rewards of the contemplative life. I was four years old when the playground was created, and at first it seemed a marvellous invention. Where there had been nothing but two square blocks of overlooked prairie in the middle of the subdivision, cluttered with crocuses and car fenders, there suddenly appeared swings, teeter-totters, monkey-bars, a slide and a sandbox, all surrounded by numberless saplings with their attendant guy wires so they would not fall over. The playground was the sensation of the neighbourhood. Long queues developed in front of each piece of apparatus, and mothers and fathers who had only the usual nodding acquaintance with other parents stood together happily while Junior and Baby Sister dutifully squealed down the slide or screamed "Look at me" from the top of the monkey-bars. As the evening wore on, the crowd turned the playground into a rough cross between a carnival and a family reunion. Fathers said knowingly that those saplings would be trees before you knew it and shook their heads in good-humoured acquiescence to time. Mothers spoke of the advantages of fresh air and laughed girlishly at the suggestion that they should try the swing. Little boys raced in ever tightening circles around the knots of people, and little girls primly retied the bows in their shoelaces. Unfortunately, as would have been the case with the carnival, no-one came to pack up the playground at the end of the week.

Parents grew bored with watching their children, and the children, with no-one to perform for, grew bored as well. As the days passed the playground became more and more deserted, strangely skeleton-like in silhouette, yet oddly finished so that you knew instinctively that it was not malleable to any imaginative process. Although the children began to realize that back alleys offered more in the way of entertainment, the playground managed to extend its popularity for two weeks longer by becoming a stage for pre-pubescent power politics.

One or another clique each evening held sway over the various pieces of playground apparatus, and each fledgling leader would, in unison with his followers, loudly proclaim the virtues of his piece of apparatus and degrade the others. There would be dirtlump fights between the Monkey-bar Faction and the Slide Faction and so forth. When such hostilities were not taking place, the leaders were content to simply demand various kinds of abasement or forfeit from anyone wishing to play on their portion of the playground. Typically, there were numberless bit-part players in the neighbourhood who were willing, even eager, to accept the role of victim, and by saying the password or providing the right sized dirtlump from the nearest excavation, have the dubious pleasure of the brief ride down the slide or turn at the swings. Not being a member of any reigning clique, and disdaining the role of victim, I was faced with either the consolations of philosophy or the excremental horrors of the sandbox. Accordingly I would observe the goings-on for a time, and then return home to the comfort of my picture books.

But even the heady exhilaration of dirtlump fights soon paled, and I noted with satisfaction that the brightly coloured contraptions that had once been so eminently attractive became more deserted. Finally one evening, a new building site lured everyone away. I came over from my customary observation point and wandered across the battlefield. Calmly, carefully, and for the first time, I tried each piece in turn. I surveyed the playground from the height of the monkey-bars. I considered its panoramic ebb and flow while swinging on the swings. I tried out the slide, both sliding down, and as I had seen the others do, attempting to walk back up the chute. Finally, I walked up the

37

inclined teeter-totter then down the other side trying to understand what had made it so attractive to everyone. Then, standing in the deepening twilight, one foot on either side of the fulcrum, balancing, I experienced the solemn affirmation of the contemplative's claim that all is vanity.

So in the spring of my twelfth year, the sudden re-emergence of the Capital Hill Tots to Teens Playground as a centre of activity surprised me. I took it in a curiously personal way, much as I would imagine Newton responding to reports of levitating apples. The transformation began in the days following the degeneration of hide-and-seek and kick-the-can because of the disappearance of the older players. I found myself associating with four other boys in the neighbourhood. Circumstances, not affection, had brought us together; even years before when I had seen through the ephemeral nature of the playground, I had been solitary in nature. Now I often wonder why I took up with them that spring. Perhaps it was simply because we were the same age and in the same grade at school. Children are great respecters of hierarchy. Perhaps we all shared the same problem of being too old and too young. In any event, I do know that Eddie, Biggs, Michael, Ralph and I all shared a similar suspense about the mystery of life even though we could not have named it at the time.

All four of us were waiting. We could have been waiting for the recreation monitor to hand out baseballs instead of soccer balls; we could have been waiting for the start or the end of marble season; the appearance of yo-yos in the store; the first crocus; the first robin; the next fight between Roger Lee and Gerald Preston; the resurfacing of Halifax Crescent; the appearance of city crews to repaint the light standards; World War Three (early that spring we had our first practise dispersal); the re-runs of a favourite television series; the organization of little league; Mr. Finnegan's first salvo in the yearly war he fought with the neighbourhood over the sanctity of his front lawn; Jackie Redding's release from the Basling, an institution where he had been sent for forcing Sidney Doberman to eat the rotten apple he had thrown at Jackie's girlfriend Trudy Nortram; the opening of the cinema that had been supposed to open in the Pacific Plaza shopping-centre sometime in the last three years; we might have been waiting for any of these things at any particular point that spring, or a hundred others, but we were not. They came and went, and we were still waiting. The twilights grew longer, but not because of the tilt of the earth. They lengthened with suspense.

It was a trying time for all of us. We started and often finished most of our evenings in front of Bronski's corner store. One of us would make a token purchase and we would sit down outside, our backs to the still warm south wall to watch the world and comment upon it. Actually it seemed more like we were waiting for some event worthy of our crow's chorus of cawing, jeering laughter. The general taste (of which I partook to a certain extent) ran toward burlesque and slapstick. I should imagine that if some old person had, out of consideration for us, slipped on a banana peel, we would have done irreparable damage to ourselves. Similarly, had there been a two- or three-car traffic accident at the corner, catapulting five or six bodies in various directions in true Keystone Cops tradition, we would have cawed and jeered and laughed and felt ourselves replete. Unfortunately, life offered very few moments with the proper lack of subtlety.

Such moments could, at considerable risk to ourselves, be induced. Joe, the Chinese gentleman who owned Bronski's corner store (the store remained Bronski's in the neighbourhood lexicon because ten years earlier a Polish gentleman had established it), could be triggered in one of two ways to do something we referred to as running amok. The first technique was to slyly pick up the price-marking stamp on Joe's counter. Various price marks such as 59¢, 75¢ and $1.85, visible on the counter-top though obviously scrubbed with great application, testified to the fact that he used some rare and indelible oriental ink for his prices. The second way to make Joe run amok was to throw a rock at the large round Coca-Cola sign on the outside wall above his door. If hit in the centre, it made a satisfying gong that reverberated in the evening air. Such actions would result in Joe rocketing out of his cluttered cubby-hole, over the counter and out the front door after Biggs, the one who was usually designated to initiate the action. We would all scatter away from him delighted and screaming at the top of our voices "Don't Spread Paper" and "No Skate Allowed." These remarks were in reference to two signs that Joe had carefully lettered. It was obvious to me he meant don't litter and don't wear ice skates in the store, but to Eddie, Ralph, Michael and Biggs, indeed to most of the neighbourhood young and old, they were the apogee of linguistic fun.

Most often we were left to content ourselves with lesser, hypothetical fare. Wouldn't-it-be-neat-if was the polysyllabic that preceded most of these options. "Wouldn't it be neat if we taped the mailbox shut and old Finnegan tried to mail a letter," one of us would say.

"Hey, Biggs, go home and get some tape," another would add.

"Naw, what's the use? He never mails a letter anyways. Who'd want a letter from him?" General laughter.

"Hey, Biggs, go over and ring McWay's bell. Wouldn't it be neat if she came out in her underwear again."

"That wasn't her underwear stupid, that was a dressing-gown."

"What do you know about underwear, Pender? You probably don't even wear underwear. Go on, Biggs, do it."

"Hey, Biggs, go across the street and pretend to pull a rope across in front of the next car."

"Nobody falls for that old one."

"Yah, I know, but Biggs doesn't. Better still just lie in the street and pretend you're hurt and when they stop and come over say thanks sucker."

"Hey, Biggs, go stamp Joe's counter."

"Hey, Biggs, why doncha ring the gong?"

We all should have been grateful to Biggs. He was the willing dupe of all our stories and the recipient of all the unused boredom and tensions that developed that spring. There were many tensions. There was no conversation, however casual, that was without a bellicose and intent probing for points of weakness. I remember one rather typical and sinister exchange that was set off by Cuthbert's fat Persian cat. It began in an argument about whether it was better to get two cats, tie their tails together and hang them over a clothesline, or simply to obtain one cat and tie a can to its tail. The conversation then progressed to the neighbourhood myth that cats who had been chased down sewers by dogs could never get out again.

Eddie, who was the leader of our particular murder of crows, claimed that once down, they were there until they died. Ralph Gabaur, displaying a previously well hidden humanity, claimed they could jump back out again. It became clear to all of us that Ralph was horrified by the vision of cats lost in the sewer. Instinctively Eddie began to exploit it.

"What do you care, Gabaur? They're just stupid cats."

"I *don't* care. I'm just saying they get out. They couldn't live down there."

"That's the whole point, Gabaur, they die down there."

Ralph was flushed and obviously agitated. He was purposefully avoiding eye contact with any of us and was throwing pebbles at the mail box.

"No, they don't."

Michael and I were staying well away from it, and even Biggs seemed to be making himself as unobtrusive as possible.

"Sure they do. They sit under the grate and meow a bit and then wander off and die. What are they gonna eat?

41

Shit?"

"How come you never see them?"

"Well, maybe you spend your time in sewers, Gabaur. I thought it was because you never took a bath."

"What was because?"

"Your smell, Gabaur." I think Eddie meant the comment to get a laugh and diffuse the situation. No-one laughed.

"I take as many baths as you Goldie, and cats don't die down there."

"Well, if you're so sure then fire one down and let's see if he gets out. Go over and get Cuthbert's cat. If he's not too fat to go in, we'll just see if he gets out."

I knew Cuthbert's Persian would never get out. He was too well-fed to even chase birds, but I was not about to interfere.

"Do it yourself, Goldie."

"Naw, I'm not the one who's all trembly about it, Gabaur. You do it."

Ralph said nothing, and Eddie, as if on cue, turned to Biggs.

"Hey, Biggs, go on over to the sewer."

"Leave him alone."

"Who? Biggs?"

"Naw, the cat. I don't give a shit about Biggs." There was no laughter, but the tension eased. Eddie, once again, followed it up.

"Hey, Biggs, look down there and tell us what you see."

"There's nothing there."

"Bend down and look closer." Biggs, ever useful, bent down and looked closer.

"Hey, what's the matter, Biggs? Didn't your old lady give you supper tonight?" There was a brief communal jeer while Biggs obligingly clowned and attempted to lift the storm drain off. We settled on our perches again.

Such were the innocent joys of boyhood, which, until that spring, I had kept at arm's length. For that matter, I have often wondered why they bothered letting me associate with them at all. I did not laugh at the right times and often I completely missed my cues in conversation. But they did respect my one and only weapon: I had a wicked tongue. In a neighbourhood where the corner grocery store was still known by the name of a man who had left ten years before, it was no mean weapon.

I had gained my skills because of the usual reason: self defence. Years before, Michael Pender's grandmother, a gossip of formidable proportions, had remarked that I spent entirely too much time at home with my picture books. She was then reported to have said, "It's no wonder Elaine Corning's little hothouse plant has no friends." Michael had passed the name around, and soon I was known throughout the neighbourhood as The Hothouse Plant or sometimes simply as Hothouse.

I discovered the hard way that there is absolutely no way to fight words. I devoted myself to becoming the most skillful bicycle rider in the neighbourhood, hoping to overcome my reputation as a stay-at-home. When that did no good I took my wood burning set and inscribed the name of "Flash" in slanting letters upon a small shingle of wood that I hung behind the seat of my bicycle; everyone still called me Hothouse. I even tried physical intimidation with some of the smaller children, but I discovered it was a physical fact that voices carried further than fists or rocks; echoing after whatever threat I made would come "Hothouse Hothouse Hothouse" in an obnoxious, childish sing-song.

I cannot be sure now that Grandmother Pender knew what she had done, but I hated her passionately nonetheless. Every summer evening she would sit on the front step of Pender's in a wicker rocking chair, rocking and keeping her eye on the neighbourhood. Every time I passed by she would call out in an evil parody of good nature, "Hello, Jonathan, read any good books lately?" She would then wrinkle her face up in a grimace of a smile. It was her wrinkled face that finally provided me with the inspiration I needed.

It seems to me now that my solution came to me out of the clear blue of the evening sky, but I was probably brooding upon my revenge for the entire three years. It happened while I was riding by on my bicycle. For perhaps the thousandth time she called out her question. Michael, who was sitting on the bottom step, called out right after her. "Yah what about it Hothouse? Read any good books?"

Without thinking I found myself slowing the bicycle down, jerking it up on its back wheel, and then swinging it around a full 180° so that I was suddenly driving back in front of the Pender's. The trick turn was amazing enough. I had seen it at the circus and had been practising it unsuccessfully for days. Michael and his odious grandmother were agog with surprise at my sudden reversal of direction, and I was only slightly less so. But what happened next transcended surprise. As if it were someone else, I heard myself calling out, "Hey Pender, your grandmother's an old raisin face." To this day I do not remember thinking up the name, but its effect was unforgettable. Grandmother Pender's eyebrows, as if detached from her face, flew rapidly up and down while her mouth opened and shut inarticulately like a poplar leaf turning in the wind. Even Michael laughed.

News that such a venerable citizen as Grandmother Pender had been so rudely addressed by an eight-year-old boy travelled rapidly through the neighbourhood. Michael's mother even phoned to complain to my mother. My reputation was assured, and for the remaining six years of her life Grandmother Pender could not sit on her porch on a summer's evening without hearing, sometimes in actuality and sometimes only in imagination, some neighbourhood child calling her Old Raisin Face. But as rare as justice is in this world, that evening satisfied me far more than simple revenge could ever have done. I had heard the billiard-ball-click of words falling neatly into place over some stubborn part of the world. It felt the way third gear felt dropping

44

into place as I pedalled downhill. All the passion I had put into bicycling and reading was suddenly directed toward my new skill.

Only two or three times did it ever approach the rightness I felt that first time. Perhaps my finest achievement came that very spring. It was a short sing-song verse designed after Mr. Finnegan had confiscated yet another baseball that had landed on his lawn. I still remember the group of boys lying on Doberman's lawn after I gave the verse to them. It was dark and looking across the street it seemed they had been scattered like breadcrumbs for birds, framed and frozen in their casual arrangement every time the headlights of a car washed over them. Then gradually, at first indistinguishable from the evening sounds of the neighbourhood and their own half-laughing half-rebellious comments, I heard it begin:

Old Mrs. Finnegan
had a hair on her chinegan
when along came a wind
and blew it back in again.

It was then repeated as more of them joined in:

Old Mrs. Finnegan
had a hair on her chinegan
when along came a wind
and blew it back in again.

And then finally from a group of boys who normally on principle would disagree about the day of the week, it rose out of the darkness in full united chorus. It may have been inane, but it was mine, and so it rose sweetly in the night air achieving the dignity of an anthem or hymn.

Old Mrs. Finnegan

45

had a hair on her chinegan
when along came a wind
and blew it back in again.

The Finnegan's front hall light came on. Mr. Finnegan stepped out on the front porch and fired one baseball, rather forcefully for an elderly man, into the night air.

Of course, what we were all waiting for finally arrived. When Barbara Hanley, Amanda Jenson and Beverly Spalden appeared upon the scene, I could find no words to explain them away. Ironically, the night they appeared was one of the best nights I ever spent with the other four boys. It was two weeks before I was to leave for Union. Eddie, Ralph, Michael and I were lying on the stack of hockey-rink boards that the city maintenance crews piled up in the middle of the playground each spring after the ice was gone. The stack was about six feet high, and while it remained, usually for about three weeks, it was a favourite spot for the children.

We were all feeling a rare contentment as we lay looking up into the sky. It was twilight, and twilight is a more distinct time for a child. If one wanted to go home, the darkness that was revealed by the glow from porch lights and kitchen windows was excuse enough. If one wanted to stay, as we did that evening, the light still up in the sky was a good enough reason.

The more immediate explanation for our contentment is that we had just successfully captured the hockey-rink boards from a larger group of neighbourhood boys. It was not mere possession that pleased us. Instead, it was the flawless execution of Eddie's plan of assault that made us content. He had sent Biggs up the front of the stack on what he termed a "suicide diversion," while the rest of us had climbed up from behind. At a pre-arranged signal, just as we all had our heads over the top, we screamed in unison. The effect had been impressive. The six boys who had been pelting Biggs with dirtlumps had, as one, leapt off the stack and ran away. The victory had been particularly pleasing to Eddie. "Not one shot fired," he had repeated two or three times, with obvious satisfaction.

The remark was revealing of Eddie and the reason why we accepted him as leader. He had a personal and strident vision of what was right and proper. For any other boy, the throwing of dirtlumps would have been the purpose of the whole exercise, but not for Eddie. For him it was the planning and the execution—the generalship—that mattered. In earlier years he had gained the dubious reputation of turning even the most casual fracas into organized mayhem. More than one child had remarked that he made a dirtlump fight seem like going to school. Somehow he always managed to convince his side to throw sequenced and devastating volleys of dirtlumps. Any combatant hit upon the arm or the leg had to retire from the battle and count to 50. Anyone hit upon the body had to count to 150 and those hit upon the head had to quit completely (although they usually did anyways). On firecracker day he made any child who enjoyed simply throwing the firecracker and waiting for the bang feel inadequate. He would be intent upon stripping the powder out of three or even four whole packages to make a bomb out of a tin can or a milk bottle. More often than not the bomb never worked, but this never deterred him.

Indeed, watching him from afar over the years, I had often wondered why anyone bothered with him at all. That spring evening I understood. When his plans worked, they really worked. It was not just a matter of who was biggest or who could shout the loudest or throw the farthest. It was not even a question of superior numbers. He provided that rarest of all childhood experiences (for that matter, for adults as well): concentrated, co-ordinated, planned effort. It was an experience I had never tasted before, and it was intoxicating.

As we lay there staring up into the deepening blue, I was making plans. Masks, I thought, would be useful for the fear they would inspire, and successful tactical exercises should be written down for future use. I thought a battle cry would be appropriate, and perhaps even passwords. I think I was creating the role of intelligence officer for myself when Michael expressed, albeit crudely, the nature of the thoughts we were all having.

"Jeez. That was great. Let's go away and if they come back we can do it again."

Eddie's reply was final, "Naw, that's for kids. We wanted it and we took it, but unless you're five years old you gotta have a reason. You have to wait for the right time to do something. You can't just do it."

Eddie's reply was as close to a philosophical comment as he had ever come, and we were all suitably impressed. Ralph made it official.

"Yeah, Pender, it's not like Joe's gong."

Michael's mistake had saved me from making the kind of mistake I feared most—speaking at the wrong time—but mentally I continued with my error. There and then, at the end of the spring, and if it is not being too melodramatic, at the beginning of the end of my innocence, I made no reservations. I knew that Eddie would come up with some even better plan, and I was content to wait. As if to confirm my trust, Michael asked where Biggs was and Eddie replied he had been hit in the face with a dirtlump and had gone home to wash his mouth out. Then, like a general granting a medal, he said, "I told him to get a quarter from his mother and pick up an order of french fries on the way back. If you go right at closing you get all they got left."

"Great," was all any of us could think of to say. It was great. I suppose I had the kind of feeling that made other children want to stay out playing football long after it was too dark to see the ball. It was the kind of feeling I had making home base in hide-and-seek, but it was better. The hockey-rink boards were warm with the heat of the day, and the smell of the dew coming on and the faint chill in the air made them seem safe and secure the way candles seemed in a power-cut. The sky above us deepened and hollowed out, and the air became clear. The first star came out and nobody laughed when Ralph Gabaur wondered whether wishing on it would really work.

There was an unspoken feeling of communion. I was suddenly hot and cool and lightheaded and clearheaded all at the same time. I rose up on one elbow and saw that all the neighbourhood lights had come on, and for the first time the suburb seemed filled with possibilities. Then, as if I had discovered some new knowledge, my whole summer spread out before me in the same way. Union, I was sure, would have many such evenings. Lying there on our platform between night and day, the future took on a fullness.

"Who needs hide-and-seek," I said. Before anyone could answer we heard the rattle of a bicycle fender coming across the playground.

Although it was dark, I could see there were three figures, and so I knew it was not Biggs. I am not sure how I knew they were girls, but I knew. Perhaps it was by their remarks. Such things as "Oh, really" and "Did he actually say that?" seemed sophisticated, as if conversation was to be enjoyed rather than endured. Their voices seemed close, as if the darkness had performed a ventriloquist's deception. All three of us watched quietly from the top of the boards, and as they came closer Eddie named them: Barbara Hanley, Amanda Jenson and Beverly Spalden.

Ralph started to say something deprecating about girls, and Eddie told him to be quiet. The old tension appeared once more. My horizon rapidly shrunk, and once again I became just one person lying on dusty boards in the middle of a playground. It was not as if the three girls were strangers. Earlier that spring and the year before they had regularly played hide-and-seek with us. The only one who seemed notable to me at all was Beverly Spalden. By hiding one night right up against the stairs, I had seen that when she counted to 100 she first pressed her gum up against our screen with her tongue. The sticky stain, which seemed to return no matter how many times it was removed, had puzzled my parents exceedingly. Although I never said anything to Beverly or my parents about it, I felt we had shared a secret.

The girls passed us and stopped at the swings, perhaps twenty yards further on. Eddie suggested in a strangely casual voice that we go down and sit on the monkey-bars. I must have still thought he had some larger plan in mind. It never even entered my head that we were going over to be near to the girls, and in the casual banter that arose between us and them I completely missed the exchange that forged the tacit agreement. I did not recall it until three days later.

It was Barbara Hanley who said, "Why don't you go someplace else. We were here first."

Eddie replied "This is a municipal playground, we will come here every night if we want to."

I suppose I should have known then and there that I was once again on my own. Nevertheless, for the following three evenings I returned with them to the playground, and each time the girls were there. What made it difficult for me is that not once did anyone say openly that we were going to the playground to meet them. Instead, all our journeys there were elaborately casual. There would be academic discussions of whether or not we should sit in front of Joe's, ride our bikes or go to the shopping centre, but reasons were always found for not doing such things, and I would find that once again we were walking over the playground toward the swings.

It was inevitable that the difference in view that had developed between myself and the others would be formally recognized. On the fourth night, when we were once again making our way to the playground with an ostentatious lack of design, I was banished. The other four were walking, but I had brought my bicycle hoping that we were going riding. I was circling around them very slowly. In fact, at points I was simply holding the bike still and balancing, a feat that sounds and looks more difficult than it really is. Perhaps it was the concentration I needed for the bicycle that led to my lapse in tactics. I asked with unfortunate logic that if we did not know what we wanted to do then why were we walking in the direction of the playground.

Eddie had just received his summer haircut and it made him seem even more formidable than usual. His father still insisted upon shaving his neck and the sides of his head right up to above his ears, leaving the top half slightly longer. It was known in the vernacular as a "bowl" haircut. It gave him a warlike appearance. Beneath the unforgiving, itchy-looking stubble on the sides and back of his head, I could see his white scalp contrasting with his dark hair above and his tanned neck below. He looked at me very coldly and made the eminently logical reply, "Why not?" I made the mistake of replying openly that they wanted to go there just because of the girls.

He was, on the whole, quite restrained. "If you don't want to come, Corning, then don't. Nobody asked you."

The troops provided the chorus. "Yah, go home and read a book." "Yah, Hothouse, go home to Mommy." "We didn't ask you anyways."

I quit balancing my bicycle and watched them move away from me. I pedalled over to the hockey-rink boards and sat there watching. For the first twenty minutes it was the cause of some comment. Eddie, out of character and probably trying to impress the girls, tried a shouted argument with me.

"Bug off, Hothouse."

"It's a free country. I can stay here if I want to."

"Didn't you hear me, Corning. I said bug off."

"I heard you, Goldie, I said I'll stay if I want. Maybe if you took that bowl off your head, you'd understand."

Knowing they were clearly bested in any verbal duel, they tried chasing me away, but on my bicycle that was useless. By the end of the evening they had decided to simply ignore me.

For the following four evenings I haunted the playground. Then, on the fourth evening, I found it deserted. I felt no vindication. I ran into Biggs a few minutes later at the corner store and I questioned him about the others. They had left, he said, because of a rumour of an incredible clubhouse that had been discovered in the bushes. The really big news was that although it was supposed to be the most fantastic clubhouse ever constructed, no-one knew precisely where in the bushes it was located. Eddie, Michael, Ralph and the girls were sitting over on the lip of the ravine, Biggs told me, along with almost the entire neighbourhood, speculating where the clubhouse was located and who had built it.

I must have been content as I pedalled toward the edge of the ravine in which the bushes were located. Although I had never actually participated in the construction of a clubhouse, I considered myself an authority on them. I was convinced that however mysterious the location of this new clubhouse might be, it could not be as formidable as the mystery of life.

I had watched the cycle of clubhouse construction from afar year after year. Christmas-tree forts were for the winter, underground forts in the vacant lot at the corner were for the spring and early summer, and in summer and early fall, leaning up against a fence or a garage or a back step, the honest - to - goodness, made - out - of - wood clubhouse appeared. From the expeditionary aura that settled on the builders at the start, to the tear-stained face of the one participant who was blackballed from the club after the excitement of the construction subsided, I understood the phenomena of clubhouses. I suppose there is something as ancient as the three little pigs involved in clubhouse construction, and in my heart I was convinced that if I ever put my hand to it, I would be the one to build the clubhouse of bricks that was proof against the wolf. I knew that this rumoured clubhouse would not be as good as the one I would make, but I was intrigued.

The bushes were an area of perhaps five square blocks that existed in the ravine between our subdivision and the next one over. The very centre of the bushes was swampy and hillocked and almost impossible to move through until midsummer when it dried out. The edges were posted with "No Dumping" signs, but the bushes were always surrounded by a zone of litter, mainly dry-fill and concrete slabs, a few old tires, broken bottles and rain-bleached newspapers. The centre of the area, the bushes proper, was comprised of densely packed willow and poplar brush, growing so thickly that it was impossible to walk upright, even for a child. There was, however, a web of small game trails that could be navigated by walking bent double. I expect the trails were used mainly by the local dogs and cats, but there could have been an occasional coyote or skunk, as well.

The bushes were the place where Ross Geller had taken refuge after robbing a milk-delivery truck. It had been big neighbourhood news. Ross had always been slightly suspect because he had a cleft palate. He was ostracized by his peers, and those of us who were younger had singled him out as an object of special interest. When he was not within hearing distance we laughed at his funny way of speaking, and then, perhaps because of guilt, we were afraid of him when he was present. In any event, he confirmed all of our suspicions about him one spring morning when he swung onto the milkman's truck brandishing a knife and demanded that the driver surrender his money. There were reports, greatly lampooned by the neighbourhood wits, that he had worn a bandanna, stagecoach robbery style, but that the milkman had recognized him by his speech difficulty. For a time it was a guaranteed laugh to approach someone and say in a slurred nasal tone. "Reach for the thky. Thith ith a thtick up Misther," or "Your milk money or your life."

Still, when it was discovered that he had been hiding out

in the bushes for a day and a half after the robbery, everyone was slightly embarrassed that they had laughed. Three police cars converged on the bushes late in the afternoon. Their red lights winked around in cinematic fashion until early evening, and the metal tones of the police loudspeaker and the static of the calls coming through on the two-way radios rang up in the clear air. Standing above the ravine and looking on, the whole neighbourhood was impressed. Pipe-smoking fathers quietly speculated that he had made a mistake in taking to the bushes and claimed that he should have disappeared downtown, gone east or acted as if nothing had happened. Mothers happily commiserated over poor Mrs. Geller, and all of the neighbourhood children raced back and forth starting rumour after rumour that Ross had been seen at this or that corner of the bushes. When he finally appeared at the edge of the bushes he had enough presence of mind to raise his hands in surrender, for which dramatic touch a small cheer went up. For weeks afterwards we all speculated that somewhere in the bushes he had cached his loot, and for years afterwards the legend persisted of treasure in the bushes.

Ross, of course, was not the only legend of the bushes. Mr. Cuthbert, whose upstairs window looked out on the area, claimed year in and year out that the place was a "Hobo Jungle" and that the city should take in bulldozers. No-one ever paid any attention to him unless there were current reports of someone escaping from one institution or another. Then the parents would look down upon the bushes suspiciously, gradually becoming convinced that any escaping lunatic or prisoner might have fled there to hide from prisons and asylums that were as distant as 400 miles away. And, of course, on a yearly basis legends of another kind would appear. One of the neighbourhood girls would be seen disappearing into the bushes with a boy, or simply be reported to have done so, and she would achieve long-lasting notoriety.

So, knowing that the bushes grew stories as abundantly as willows and discarded automobile tires, I was fairly skeptical of Biggs' story of a marvellous construction located there.

By the time I arrived, most of the non-adult population had assembled at the edge of the ravine. Eddie and the others were sitting off to one side. I was unsure about what their reaction to me would be, but I did not need to worry because just then a relatively rare event took place. Gary Burns and Mary-Elizabeth Cummings arrived arm in arm and with them were Jeffrey Haines, Robert Skeller and Debbie Bender. Gary and Mary-Elizabeth must have been all of fifteen or sixteen years old, but for us they had all of the glamour and none of the drawbacks of adults. They announced that they were going to roast potatoes and that anyone who wanted to had better go home and get their own. We all did. Roasting potatoes happened only once or twice a season, and it was a prized event.

By the time I rode back with my potatoes and envelope of salt, the pit had already been dug and the fire started. I could tell even as I was getting off my bicycle that in the presence of Gary and Mary-Elizabeth the usual taboos and antagonisms had been relaxed. The girls were sitting with the boys around the fire, and the factions that usually kept well apart, the Ritt brothers and Eddie, for example, had been disregarded for the evening like the informal truces made by soldiers on Christmas Eve.

Talk had already begun about the mysterious clubhouse in the bushes. With the fire burning and the sparks rising it was as if everyone was allowed to speak in ways that were not normally permitted. When there was laughter it was good natured and not derisive. I had noticed the same thing happen on other, similar occasions. It was not as if people became different, but more as if some essence in each personality was allowed freer rein. When I sat down, Ralph Gabaur was in the middle of speculating about the rumour.

"It could be anyone down there. That's all I am saying. It could be..." He paused. Most of us knew what he was going to say. He was going to suggest that there could be war criminals hiding in our bushes. Eddie nudged Biggs, and Biggs snickered. Ralph was fascinated with war criminals. His father had been in the German army during the war, and once or twice when he had drunk too much, he had lined up the neighbourhood boys and lectured them about the war and how close Germany had been to victory. I expect Ralph had been lectured in a similar fashion more than just once or twice, but the effect of Mr. Gabaur's war stories was not what he had anticipated. Instead of taking pride in his German heritage, Ralph had instead become fascinated with war criminals. He knew all about them, both the Germans and the Japanese. Finally he came out with it. "It could be war criminals down there."

"Maybe it's Hitler himself," was Eddie's contribution. Before anyone could guffaw, Gary interrupted.

"Well you know, that could be right. I was reading the other day that they never really got positive proof that Hitler was killed, and a lot of Nazis did escape to South America. I guess some of them could have come up here." Gary acted the role of arbitrator rather well. "The question is how did they get in our little patch of bush?"

Being taken seriously, Ralph lost his usual sullen expression and offered us his theory. "Just say they were working as ranch hands in the mountains and someone figured out they were Nazis. They could have come down the river and up to the bushes. They could be hiding there until they arranged for false papers."

With the coals shifting and glowing, his theory was almost plausible. Everyone took their turn. Amanda Jenson said it might be "little people" and upon being questioned told of how her grandmother had met a little person who lived in a hole in the ground in Lithuania. "And maybe, just maybe," she finished, "they might live over here too."

Someone suggested gypsies, someone suggested squatters, and the coals glowed, and the stars came out, and we ate our potatoes, remarking repeatedly that they always tasted best when roasted in a fire.

I offered no theory of my own. As I sat there, feeling the still warm concrete slab behind my back and the night breeze fresh on my face after the heat of the fire, I made plans for the following day. I decided I would go down and walk through the bushes until I found whatever was there. Whether it was a band of leprechauns, war criminals, squatters or gypsies, I would know. Indeed, even if it was just Andy Wontner taking Janie Cormack to some place private in the bushes, then I would know that too. There would be no mystery for me. I felt somehow older than the others. It felt sad to be standing away from the fire and thinking such thoughts. After a time, one by one, they started to leave. I took one last look at the bushes and then followed them.

The next morning the whole situation looked different. I dismounted from my bicycle on the lip of the ravine and stood there for a moment looking down at the bushes and deciding where to begin my search. I had decided to use a technique I had learned in Mark Trail that involved orienting myself by the sun and criss-crossing the whole area at intervals of about fifteen yards. It was a rather prosaic way to treat the mystery of the bushes, but I knew it would be effective. The night before, the adventure had seemed noble, almost heroic, but standing there I began to feel irritable. I wondered why it had been left to me to make the search. It occurred to me that if they really thought there were war criminals or small people or even Andy Wontner and Janie Cormack, then they should have been all down there themselves instead of sitting around a fire and talking about it.

By the time I had made the third pass through the bushes, keeping the sun to my left, I had ceased to think about anything. It was hard work. I had an itchy spiderweb feeling on my face and hands. My sneakers were soaked and my feet felt slimy. Wandering in the winding, branching pathways, bent over double and emerging in a corner of the bushes completely opposite to where you thought you were going to emerge was one thing; methodically pushing through each and every bush and keeping to a straight line was an entirely different matter. I suppose I took some satisfaction that Mark Trail's tip worked. Each time I emerged I was fifteen yards further down the length of the bushes. That feeling of satisfaction, however, was overruled by a growing disillusionment. The bushes were not the impenetrable wilderness they had seemed to be. Even well toward the centre, one or two abandoned tires could be found, undoubtedly rolled from the lip of the ravine. The green tunnels that had previously been the only way of navigating through the ravine no longer seemed to promise secret destinations. I realized for the first time that I could hear cars going by and neighbourhood lawnmowers droning back and forth. I began to feel foolish and angry. I began to hope that I could at least encounter some anomaly, even a skunk, that would commemorate my effort. I thought of Ross Geller, but my disillusionment was so complete that I did not think of his hidden cache of money. Instead, I felt a tired compassion for him, and a curious envy that at least he was able to walk out of the bushes reaching for the sky in honourable surrender.

Still, I continued. There was no stealth or woodcraft in my movement; it was simply a matter of doggedly climbing through or over or under every obstacle in my path. When I actually walked into one wall of the clubhouse, my first impulse was ludicrous. I glanced quickly around to see if anyone had seen me blunder into it; it was as if I had been caught singing a foolish song or dancing a jig. My next reaction was equally ludicrous. All of the notions of war criminals and little people came to me, and I rapidly decided the appropriate response was to backtrack in my own steps and reconnoitre the area. I am not quite sure why this seemed appropriate; it was, after all, a technique supposedly used by Indians to foil enemies who were tracking them. I did it, nevertheless, and it seemed to go some way toward restoring my self respect. I reconnoitred for about five minutes, trying to think of some other properly cunning action before I finally admitted to myself that there was no-one around, and furthermore, that if the owners did show up they would not be little people or war criminals or any of the other possibilities I had prepared myself for. I tried to feel excited. I tried to feel fearful. I tried to feel elated. I was completely unsuccessful with each in turn.

Squishing slightly in my wet running-shoes, I walked slowly up to it. It was absolutely different from anything I had been prepared for; it was perfect. It was perfect the way that other clubhouses were never perfect. It was the way things were when I imagined them while reading about them in stories. It was pretend taken to its logical extreme, or perhaps it was something done so well that pretend was not needed. The walls were made out of woven branches. The builder had found four willow bushes growing in a rough square, and he, or she, had simply bent the branches and woven them together. One or two of the larger branches had been tied down in place with twine, and some of the lower branches had been bent until they had broken. Those that were broken had no leaves upon them; I realized that construction had taken place in the previous summer.

I walked around it until I found the entrance, bent down and entered. Discarded boards and an old road sign had been laid down on two-by-fours to make a dry level floor. The road sign was a DO NOT ENTER, and it had been put down right at the entrance way. The inside walls had been woven with branches that had been cut and brought in. The weaving was close, like a wicker-work chair or a basket. There was nothing left of the inside furnishings except for two items. The first was a simple square of burlap that was

59

tied off to one side of the entrance way. It was like a curtain. I untied it and hooked it over the entrance. A huge X was embossed upon it. Bottle caps had been used. The cork from each cap had been lifted and then re-inserted into the cap with the burlap in between. I had seen children put bottle caps on their shirts in a similar fashion and wear them as badges, but the effect of the large number fastened to the curtain was like that of an embossed shield or a coat of arms. I carefully tied the curtain back. The caps were becoming rusty. The other fixture was on the other side of the hut. It was a rope hammock. For some reason I knew that it had been hand-knotted by the same person who had embossed the curtain. It was beautifully done with reef knots, each flat and precise. Like Goldilocks with the Baby Bear's bed, it was just my size, but I could not lie down in it. Spiders had recognized its excellence and had webbed many portions of it over. It was woven with bits of twigs and the irridescence of flies' wings.

I felt a momentary regret that I could not try the hammock out, and that was followed by a sudden and overwhelming regret that I did not know the builder. I knew that no-one in our neighbourhood would ever have taken such care, and I knew that no-one in our neighbourhood would ever have kept it such a perfect secret. I did not know if the builder was ten years old or fourteen, or if he was a he, or she was a she. Still, I felt a kinship with the person and a sadness for whatever had made him or her abandon such a perfect clubhouse.

I left. I pushed through the bush until I came across the first open path and followed its winding progress until I found myself stepping out into the open once more. Without pausing to look back I made my way up to the lip of the ravine and sat down beside my bicycle. It was only then that I looked back down and realized I could not even say with assurance where in the bushes it was. There was no connection between where I was sitting on the lip of the ravine and where I had been. It was a complete non-sequitur.

As if on cue, Eddie and Ralph walked by, and Ralph called out and asked what I was doing. I looked at them for a moment trying to think how to describe what I had seen, and I realized that to attempt it would be worse than useless. I tiredly confirmed my reputation as Hothouse by saying that I did not feel well and was going home. When I got home I went to my room and slept. When I awoke I could have thought the whole thing was a dream except for the scolding I received from my mother for the condition of my clothes.

And so everything returned to what it had been before the ravine, and we all returned to the playground. I told myself that if I waited long enough, the attraction of the playground would turn out as it had before, but although I did not admit it, I knew I was facing a different situation. I badly wanted to understand it.

Those last evenings progressed in an almost ceremonial fashion. I would gaze over at the monkey-bars, the swings and the teeter-totters to where the three girls were studiously ignoring Eddie, Ralph, Michael and Biggs as they performed feats of strength and daring. They would climb the pole supports of the swings and dangle from the cross bar; they would clamber up the chains the swings hung from; and they would swing the seats around and around the cross bar until they dangled six feet off the ground. Each evening, when they had finished doing everything to the swings except swing on them, they would begin to tease the girls. As on the first night, the sound of the voices seemed to jump up out of the twilight as if not earth bound.

"Oh, don't be so childish," the girls would say, and the four boys would echo them with a shrill falsetto, "Oh, don't be so childish, so childish, so childish." Looking over at them I would decide that it was, indeed, all very childish, and I would turn away and look over toward the city centre.

It was not the kind of mystery I read about in stories.

There were no hidden doors or secret stairways. But each evening, as I gazed off over the city, a feeling very like mystery would descend. The row upon row of houses that I could see from my vantage point would become shadowed and undifferentiated, even less interesting than they were in full daylight. But then, somewhere in some power station, a clock would tick the streetlights on, and row after row of lights would flicker into sight. It was like a huge puzzle being put together, but the playground had no streetlights, so the puzzle would remain unsolved. Awakening to the darkness, we would all straggle home.

The mystery continued to grow until two days before my departure to Union when word of the Mermaid percolated through the neighbourhood. I first heard of her at the playground. Michael described her to the others.

His description was basic. "She's got 'em out to here." He cupped his hands at arm's length in front of his chest. "The biggest anyone's ever seen, and she's naked. Right there in Castleman's backyard. They painted her on the bottom of the pool." The boys laughed knowingly, and the three girls expressed appropriate shock.

The complete story, as I discovered next day, was only slightly less cryptic. The Castlemans had painted a mermaid on the bottom of the cement lily pond in their backyard. There was, however, great disagreement about her appearance. Some said she had clothes on, while others said she wore nothing at all. Some claimed she was not a mermaid, but simply a naked woman. There was even one rumour, whispered in hushed voices, that it was in fact a painting of Mrs. Castleman with no clothes on.

The reason for the rumours was simple. The Castlemans were not fond of children, and they had a six-foot high fence around their yard to keep everyone out. As I think back on it now, there was a certain pathos in the scene behind Castleman's fence. Three short lines of neighbourhood children, mostly boys but there were a few girls, were waiting patiently for their turn to chin themselves on the Castleman's fence and peer through the trees at the pond for as long as they could sustain their own weight. Each one would scrabble at the smooth surface of the fence in an attempt to stare longer. Incongruously, it seemed that as they stared down into the pond, they were treading water. When it was my turn I discovered it was all for nothing more than the vaguest hint of form and colour that could be seen below the water.

Still, I understood immediately. She was not the mystery of the abandoned clubhouse. She was tangible. In a suburb of straight lines, she had curves. In a climate of hints and guesses, she had form. At a time when the mystery of life was intangible, she was real. Then and there I resolved to come back that evening, climb over the fence and peer directly into the water.

That evening, as I listened to Eddie and the others tease the girls, I felt a special kind of superiority; I was going to perform a feat that none of them had dared. And with the feeling of superiority was a loneliness; I was going to see what they only told stories about, but I knew they would not even notice when I left early.

I made my way to Castleman's backyard and climbed over the fence. Before I walked over to the pond, I believe I stopped and thought about climbing back out. Then, as I walked toward her, I wondered what she would be like; if she was really a mermaid; if she was clothed; if she was naked; perhaps even if she was Mrs. Castleman. But most of all, I wondered if she would give me an answer.

The fence and trees and shrubs shadowed the yard. The sun had gone down, but the sky was reflected in the water, making the pond a pool of brightness. The yard sprinkler had been on so the leaves and the grass gleamed with drops of water. I swung into the yard on the branch of a flowering tree and the white petals had stuck to my shoes and pant legs where they were damp. When I reached the pool I held onto a poplar that was growing beside it so that I could lean out and look down. I remember that its trunk had been scored, probably when they had excavated for the pond, and for a moment I was taken aback by the smooth firmness where the bark was peeled away. There was a dry stickiness from the sap.

Did I see her as she really was? Did I see a cartoon caricature of a mermaid, buxom and brightly coloured, yet blurred by the water as if she had been copied from the Saturday funny papers after they had been left on the porch overnight and smeared by the dew? Or was she some brassy, slick, confident creature whose top half had been taken from a cigarette ad and whose bottom half had been taken from a tuna fish commercial? Or was she a middle-aged man's dream of beauty, her skin so impossibly white that past her breasts—down over her navel and the rise of her hips—it took on the faint blue of the whitest of snows before—even lower and more mysterious—it became the deep blue, the irridescent shimmer of never-seen-before, never-to-be-seen-again scales that winked with a memory of the sea? Now I like to think that some chance current waved her hair back from her breasts and opened her arms in welcome for me, but perhaps I simply lost myself in the glint and gleam of deep water and imagined what I needed to see.

Later, the light faded from the pool and I walked wearily home and sat upon the back porch. I remember sitting and watching the flowers in the garden. Colour by colour they seemed to light up in the twilight and then disappear. First the lilacs and the deeper reds, and then finally, in the unkempt corners the yellow dandelions blazed then faded. My questions were unanswered, the mystery was intact, but there was a strange aftertaste in my mouth, flat and faintly stale. It stayed with me the next day on my journey to Union.

Stop! O Thief Time

On arriving in Union, I discovered that I was going to have to contend with my grandfather full time. I knew that he had sold the hardware store to George Maclenan the previous fall. The story I did not know, and which I put together from bits and pieces during those first few days in Union, was that in the middle of January Mr. Maclenan had banished my grandfather from the store, forbidding him to set foot in it ever again unless it was for a specific purchase.

The root of the problem was my grandfather's love of talk. The hardware store had given him the opportunity to expound upon politics, the price of beef, freight rates, the weather, the condition of the crops, what old Mr. Swartz the butcher tried to pass off as hamburger, or any other topic that was, for him, currently interesting. It was assumed by the townspeople that part of the purchase price of any article in the store was the payment of at least five minutes of close attention to my grandfather's views. In all fairness, I expect that many of the farmers enjoyed the chance to catch up on current events. Of course, current events were not his only sphere of interest. By the time I was eleven, I had heard him argue everything from the authenticity of the Bible to the proper methods of education for young children.

When he sold the store to George Maclenan, he had mistakenly assumed that he had retained the story rights. He had continued to go down around ten o'clock for coffee, and sometimes he had returned for the afternoon break as well. Coffee at the hardware store had been a tradition that he established with a few of the neighbouring merchants as well as a few other townspeople who showed up on a regular basis. They had developed the habit of sitting down on the long wooden counter, the nail kegs or whatever else was handy, and spending half an hour to 45 minutes drinking coffee and talking. Grandfather's personal sessions probably started to lengthen around November, and by December he was often spending an entire morning there. The only problem was that people were no longer listening to him quite as attentively as they had when it had been his coffee and his store. At this point, I know that he must have resorted to his usual tactics.

He was a guerilla fighter. No ploy was too subtle or too obvious. His only criteria seemed to be whether or not it drew attention to whatever he was saying or about to say. I can recall many of his tactics, ranging from simply speaking in a very loud voice to making barely audible asides whenever anyone else was talking, but the technique that tantalized me most was his use of the cigar ashes. He smoked at least two cigars every day, one in the early evening just after supper, and one later on just before the eleven o'clock news, and he smoked them impeccably. He smoked while sitting in the chair in the corner of the front room by the window. The sunlight would be coming in, or the lamplight would be shining so that before he was through all that could be seen to indicate that he was still there behind the swirls of smoke were the gleams of light that reflected from his bald head or his steel-rimmed reading-glasses. Of course, I always knew he was there, staring out keenly, and probably smugly aware that the smokescreen gave his pronouncements the effect of an oracle.

He always began the same way. He would set the box on the lamp table beside the chair and lift the lid so that the woman on the box looked at everyone for perhaps two minutes. Finally, he would clear his throat, and as if it had just occurred to him, he would make his announcement.

"Well, they're no good to look at and they're no good to eat. Guess I might as well burn one up."

Although it had been abundantly obvious for five minutes that he was going to smoke a cigar, it still served his purpose because my grandmother would stop whatever she was doing and with a resigned voice make her reply. I do not know what she said when I was not there, but when I was there it was always the same.

"Oh, Rod. Not while Jonathan is here."

"I'm sorry Ruby. Am I forgetting my manners? What about it Johnny? Care for one?"

"Don't you listen to him Jonathan. It is a filthy habit and it weakens the will."

"What do you say Johnny? Quarter a piece. You might as well start with the best."

I knew that silence would do me no good, so I would reply at the first opportunity. "No, sir. But thank you anyways."

But, in actual fact, I did want one. Intensely. I would watch the unwrapping of the cigar, the sniffing of it and the moistening of it with great attention. But the real mark of his artistry was that he would let the ash on the end of it grow to great lengths. The effect this had upon my grandmother was truly impressive. At about an inch, she would begin glancing nervously in his direction, looking up from her work or away from whoever she was speaking to. At an inch and a half she was compelled to speak.

"Rod, if that ash falls on the floor I will not clean it. It's bad enough that you put the smoke in the air, but ash on the floor is inexcusable."

If he were feeling peaceful that night, he would take the cigar out of his mouth, look at the ash as if in surprise, and with a show of regret, lean over and carefully break the ash off, leaving it sitting like a miniature wasps' nest on the ashtray. "It filters the air, Ruby, cools the smoke, but rather than have you worry..." If, however, there was company, and the conversation was particularly interesting, he would let the ash grow and grow and treat every one of Grandmother's complaints as an invitation to offer his views on the points being discussed.

When he let the ash grow, the tension was almost unbearable for me. He would look at the end of his cigar with each complaint, weigh its fate in the balance, and then return it to his mouth. His perusal of the whorls of ash was so intent that I would become completely involved, afraid that it would fall off and crumble, and yet also anxious that he would let it grow to the longest possible length.

Even with the cigar completely finished, he managed to squeeze one last bit of use from it. His ashtray was one of those that stood on its own stand and had a plunger that when pushed, would whirl down like a top so that the ashes would fly down into the lower bowl. He would line three or four of the grey segments of ash on the tray (or even just two if there had been company) and slowly reach toward the plunger. I imagine that I did something satisfactory, like quickly draw in my breath or stiffen, and from behind the light-filled smoke would come something like a chuckle. He would make me explain centrifugal force or spell the word before he would let me press down the plunger. The one or two times that his cigar was interrupted by some arrival or departure, I went over to attempt to take one of the segments away. Always, just as they seemed about to lift up, they would crumble.

So, the root cause of his problem with George Maclenan was probably simply a matter of being too successful at gaining attention. Rumour had it that George Maclenan was having difficulty and his business was failing. There was even the suggestion that the inventory was wrong in some way because of Grandfather's idiosyncratic bookkeeping techniques. In any event, in the middle of one morning in the middle of January, when my grandfather was engaged in a particularly long and involved story of his early exploits in a west coast lumber camp and had lured away a farmer who had been negotiating for a roll of barbed wire, Mr. Maclenan finally had enough. The town's version had him being very blunt.

"Bullshit. I have had enough bullshit in here. Those tired old stories you tell are bullshit and this is a place of business.

This is not the Union Café and this is not your front room. This is a hardware store, and I own it. Next time you come in here you better come to buy."

And so my grandfather was banished, and whether or not the situation could have been saved by further discussion was never established. The lines were drawn and various versions of what had occurred were sent out to do battle in the ears of the town. The most important result of this banishment for me was that everywhere I went in the house during the first two days in Union, my grandfather was either there before me or shortly thereafter. It was awkward. I was too old for parcheesie and snakes-and-ladders and he was not quite sure what to do with me. I began to feel harried. It was like trying to have a meditative meal with an overly attentive and highly eccentric waiter hovering around the table. I sympathized with George Maclenan.

Furthermore, although I did not openly admit it, doubts about Union's ability to resist change had begun to appear. I wondered if my grandmother truly did polish the walnuts; perhaps they had simply absorbed the odour of lemon oil from the much-polished dining-room. There was no mistaking that the peppermints still tasted faintly of mothballs, but I suspected it was a condition of staleness and not enchantment. Suddenly, the jackass was no longer lewd and lascivious so much as he was old, piebald with green splotches, and even faintly ridiculous. But the things that had disappeared were only qualities and not the articles themselves, so I could artfully ignore their absence. Perhaps it was only by a curiously conscious effort of thought that I could make the roses in the glass globe shimmer back and forth between petal and porcelain, but it could be done. Similarly, I knew that the small puckers in the globe of the world in the hallway were simply the result of steam from the hot baths in the adjacent bathroom, but by a mind-stilling marathon of turning and treadling, I could force myself into a stupour where it was possible to imagine that

69

the earth, with all its hills and seas and valleys, still turned at my fingertips. In short, for the first three days in town, I singlehandedly preserved the enchantment of Union, but the spell of memory was weakening.

The weather helped me in my attempt to freeze time. It was hot and dry. The sun had created a strange effect; it had dried the spring as if it were a pressed flower. The long banner-shaped puddles that collected in the ruts at the soft edges of the street, while they no longer reflected the sky as they did in the spring, had in some ways been perfectly preserved. They had been dried so quickly that the leaves and twigs and even a few of the small water bugs that had floated there had become mired in the mud and then pinned to the dried clay. The drying had continued, cracking the clay until the multitude of tiny fractures made the bottom of each puddle resemble the dried canvas of an Old Master. It was the same with the whole of Union. The rising dust turned it into the musty warehouse of some stage company specializing in productions about small towns. The props lined the streets in perfect preservation; Swartz' Meat Market, the Lux Theatre, the Blacksmith Shop, the Union Hotel with its enigmatic Ladies and Escorts, the three grain elevators off to the side, the railroad station; even the leaves, shrunken by the heat and covered with dust, seemed to have the slight gold tinge of new spring growth so that at first glance you could not tell if it was the start of July or a dull day at the end of May.

As well, in my grandparents' house time was given the respect it deserved. Each piece of furniture, each knick-knack, having avoided being thrown out for so many decades, had a special air of artifact about it. Setting the mantelpiece clock by the national time signal was a ritual for my grandfather. Grandmother used to say—with a certain clock-like regularity herself—that he could be three days in his coffin and still rise to the sound of the tone. Her words were strangely prophetic because all during the final winter of his life he would rally slightly at eleven and ask after the clock. When he finally died, six years after that summer's visit, it was near eleven o'clock; the national time signal may have been still ringing.

But above all else, what placed Union in a time zone of its own was the way in which the walls of my grandparents' house were decorated. My grandmother's parents had imbued her with the notion that "bare walls mean bare minds." Although she had come west at the age of thirteen, she always remembered the portraits that had hung on the walls of her grandparents' home. There had been her great-grandparents, her grandmother and her father, each framed, she used to say, with gilt as thick as frosting on a bakery cake. Of course, my grandfather would have been delighted to have had his portrait painted and hung in the front room, but there were no painters in Union capable of anything but houses. So, with the oft-praised resourcefulness of the pioneer, my grandmother framed reproductions of paintings of great historical moments. They may not have been originals, and they may not have been her ancestors except in the largest sense, but it was as close as she could come. Offhand I can recall The Death of Socrates, The Death of Montcalm, The Death of Wellington and The Death of Nelson; they all seemed roughly interchangeable. There was also The Signing of the Magna Carta, The Tennis Court Declaration, Washington Crossing the Delaware, The Rape of the Sabine Women, The Last Stand of Bright's Fusiliers and innumerable other Deaths, Battles and otherwise immortal moments. Even now when I point out some distant object, I must mentally check myself against Balboa on the Darien Peninsula, or Columbus, emaciated, one hand on the wheel and his hair blown back, the caption beneath reading, "O Land! Sweet Land!"

On the second day of that summer's visit to Union, I realized for the first time that the front-room walls should have been literally papered over with immortal moments, but such was not the case. At any one time there was never more than a grand total of six. When I asked my grandmother about it, she took it as a sign that I had finally become interested in Art (she capitalized the word whenever she spoke it). She led me into her bedroom, and treating me partly like a fellow art connoisseur who had been unaccountably stranded in Union, and partly like a neighbour lady who had just asked for the secret ingredient of her turkey stuffing, she carefully opened her closet door.

From high upon the top shelf, from amongst all the other tissue-papered, perfume-scented, boxed mysteries, she took down a sheaf of what seemed like thousands of great historical moments; I later calculated that there must have been 382 of them. The paper was so thick that it rattled like sheet metal, and although it had once been white, it had antiqued to a rich cream colour, all the while holding its glossy sheen. She placed them on the bed, and then, like a fortune teller, she spread them out with a sweep of her hand. They had aged like oriental carpets; their colours had grown richer rather than fading. Many of my old favourites must have been there, but all I could see was the confusion of colour splashed upon the bedspread. I had a strange wheels-within-wheels feeling that standing there, struck dumb by the hundreds of historic moments before me, I was somehow experiencing an historic moment myself and that somewhere just out of sight someone was making a preliminary sketch of the scene.

When I finally looked up to my grandmother, she simply smiled and gestured toward the closet door. The calendar pinned to the inside of the door told the whole story. Out of a certain perversity I still order my yearly calendar from the same company so I can accurately quote the small advertisement at the bottom of the page.

Eternal Moments, one for each month of the year! The whole family can learn history and art appreciation at the same time! For the price of one calendar you receive the world's greatest art and civilization's finest moments. As well we have provided space below each date so you can mark down your personal eternal moments.

Frame your favourites! On the back of this calendar find details on how you can order our custom-made frames for those Eternal Moments that are too good to take down!

Below the current Eternal Moment there were the usual stocky black and red numerals. As the advertisement suggested, the dates had been annotated by my grandmother. The birthdays and anniversaries of all her sons and daughters and grandchildren were noted down in carefully written script. ("A fine hand shows a fine mind" was another maxim given her as a child.) There were a few names I could not place—probably second cousins—and there was even one death: "Flowers for John." John had been their youngest son, the one who was to be a painter. Although he had died over 25 years before, there he was beneath his own eternal moment. He seemed suddenly present in the room.

I went back to the bed, sat down beside my grandmother, and stared down at the swath of eternal moments. They were vibrant with the excess of colour usually found only in toy advertisements at Christmas, but it was not their colour alone that held me, because just then I knew that if I returned to the closet door and turned to the month of my birth I would find my own name noted down. Even more, I realized that somewhere on the bed was the eternal moment that had been hanging up on the day I was born. It was as if someone new and strange was paying attention to me like at the carnival when the man would look closely at you—the way that adults very rarely did—and then, with a frown of concentration, guess your age. The sense that I was in my own Eternal Moment grew even stronger.

As if to confirm my realization that each picture carried

with it its own unique set of circumstances, my grandmother began to speak. In her hand she was holding what I
would now guess to be a Bruegel's. It was some sort of har-
vest festival in the main street of a small village, and numerous squat, red-trousered villagers were making merry. It
seemed she was speaking more to herself than me. She had
her reading-glasses on to see the picture more clearly, and
her voice had reached full, interrupted gear.

"That was the September that we bought the separator...-
just like it was yesterday... The first year we got any price
for wheat... The women used to come by just to see... Of
course, Rod hadn't planted wheat that year...barley, he
said, barley was the thing.... He sold Molly to buy that separator. My, but she was a sweet old thing.... Never took to
Rod though... Neighbour would start to talk about the
price of wheat and he'd just take him out and show him the
separator.... Forget the wheat, he'd say, I've got something
you should see out in the barn...I always thought that's why
he bought it. But it worked. No-one talked about wheat
when they saw it.... My, how the ladies looked and looked-
...and the heads so heavy that year it almost looked like
some places had been hailed out."

Her rambling was even more interior than usual, and I
was about to return to the closet door when I saw The Death
of Socrates hanging above the bed. I realized that of all the
eternal moments that had hung in the house, The Death of
Socrates had been above their bed for as long as I could
remember. I interrupted her to ask her about it.

"Oh that," she said. "Your grandfather chose that one.
Said it helped his rest. He calls it Socrates' Nightcap. You
know his sense of humour. Besides, if I took it down I knew
he would put up one of his."

"One of his?" But I was already putting the pieces
together.

"Oh yes, there on the kitchen wall. At first he wanted one
in each room."

Before I could even phrase the next question, she anticipated me and continued.

"Yes, they were calendars too. Vulgar things. He had
them made up in '48 for the Hardware. He said it was for
advertising, but he did it just to spite me. They are no better than the coloured comics you children read. Still, at least
I kept them out of the front room. They are not Art,
Jonathan, that is for certain. Well, I have to go and start
supper. You take all the time you want. I'll call up when the
table is set."

At the time, the distinction between my grandfather's
and grandmother's calendars escaped me. They were both
splashed with the same Christmas-catalogue colour, and
they both had the same sense of time about them as if the
calendars that had been removed from the bottom were still
faintly visible in the same way that you can see where a picture has hung after being taken down. Of course, now that
my taste is more refined, I understand why she found them
to be something less than art. My grandfather's pictures
were clearly in the Norman Rockwell genre, although they
were not actual reproductions of Rockwell. There were four
of them hung in a row above the kitchen table, and each of
them portrayed a season. The same cast of characters was
present in all of them. There was a snowy-haired, rosy-
cheeked grandmother, a craggy-faced, not unhandsome
grandfather and four children who between them had cornered the market on freckles, pigtails, untied shoelaces, cow
licks and bright eyes.

In each picture they were performing some rite appropriate to the season. Summer, for instance, revealed Grandpa
leaning on a NO SWIMMING sign while Grandma
unpacked a picnic lunch and the three boys frolicked in the
water. In the foreground, the little girl with the pigtail was
having her bathing-suit pulled at by a small tousle-haired
dog so that part of her untanned and innocent buttock was
revealed. They were all clearly enjoying themselves, even

75

the dog. In fall, winter and spring they in turn burned leaves, skated and flew a kite. It seemed they could be uniformly jolly regardless of the season or the event. I could, of course, describe each picture in great and sarcastic detail, but when my grandmother left me I felt anything but sarcastic. Outside, the evening was coming on, but for me there were only the Eternal Moments spread around me, the seasons dancing in my head, the stocky red and black numerals of the calendar, and as if superimposed over it all, the spiderweb of my grandmother's notations.

The ballerina comes to me now, and perhaps I saw her even then. On my grandmother's chest of drawers was a bottle of liquor that had been given to her on her wedding day. It had been sent to her by an uncle who lived in Europe. As a rule strong liquor was not permitted in the house, but the bottle had been kept because of her uncle and because of a small ballerina who danced each time the bottle was lifted. A mechanism in the base of the bottle played music—"The Blue Danube Waltz"—and while it played the tiny, beautifully formed dancer would pirouette around and around inside a glass dome on the bottom of the bottle. Best of all, when the bottle was tipped upside down and then right again, flakes of gold would flutter down through the liquor, gliding silently down and around her glass bubble.

Although the bottle had never been opened, nearly a third of the liquor evaporated over the years, and because of being turned over so many times, the top part of the bottle was covered with a cloudy white residue. The gold flakes seemed to issue from a lowering cloud. Still for close to half a century, with simply a turn of the wrist, the ballerina had danced while time and gold flakes had swirled about her. I was not aware that each time she danced the residue increased and she came closer to obscurity; I thought my grandmother had forbidden me to touch her simply out of fear of my clumsiness.

And so, for those first few days after I arrived in Union, I was fully determined to resist time, change and the mermaid; as Grandfather once remarked, when you are young, you can never smell winter in the ripened fruit. Now I like to think of my younger self heroically holding up one hand and saying, "Stop! O Thief, Time," or some other appropriately bold remark, but in truth, I did not realize what I was attempting.

Still, on the morning of the third day in Union, I received a clear omen of the coming summer. Along with the heat, Union was visited by an Old Testament plague of beetles. They could be seen shuttling along any available horizontal surface, but however actively they clacked about, they froze upon being approached or even looked at directly. Because they were always moving while in the periphery of your vision but stock-still when you looked right at them, they were the objects of continual, nervous attention. Even my grandfather, who took delight in being "practical" where others were squeamish, shortened or lengthened his stride to avoid them, and more than once, upon turning to look at one and seeing it freeze, he remarked, "I wish you little sons of bitches would either fish or cut bait."

They were about the size of 50¢ pieces with three legs pointing out symmetrically from each side of their circumference. They had a tantalizing aura of wealth about them. Shiny and black, they should have been the counters in some exotic board-game, each apparently manufactured to the same specifications and from the same semi-precious stone. In fact, I am sure that in the archives of every house in Union—shelves below basement stairs or in back porches— are dusty jars in the bottom of which two or three beetles, desiccated but still shiny, bear witness to their own attractiveness. But the fact that in each jar there are only two or three points out the problem they created. They should have been collectable and useful for trading or gambling like marbles or baseball cards or even pretty rocks, but even the most avid collector among the town's offspring soon gave up. Had there been some differences between the beetles—if some had been shinier or larger than others—then relative value would have been perceived and brisk trade could have started. But they were identical. Had they been rarer, some enterprising child could have cornered the market and used them as currency to purchase goods and services from the rest. But there were so many that even the smallest child could collect dozens. But still, because of their numbers, their habits of movement and their basic beauty, no-one, young or old, could walk down the street without stooping at least once to admire their workmanship.

The morning of the third day, as my grandfather and I walked downtown through the eleven o'clock heat, it was as if we were walking over hundreds of symmetrically shaped splashes of roofing tar. As we neared the Lux Theatre three boys appeared from around the side of the building. Their eyes were on the ground and every few steps one or another would stop, pick up a beetle and deposit it in a jar. I had noticed them the evening before, moving up and down the street with the same arrogant concentration. Whatever it was they were doing, it was important, or at least they thought so. Even Grandfather was impressed by their intensity because we stopped and watched as they approached. Eyes to the ground, they did not even notice us waiting there.

I was apprehensive about meeting them. My playground experiences were still fresh in my mind. I knew the first meeting could set the tone for the entire summer. The last thing I needed was yet another nickname. Twice my grandfather had offered to take me out and introduce me, and twice—wisely as it turned out—I had demurred. I had worried that he would say the wrong things.

It was clear which boy was the leader. The other two wanted to run ahead excitedly, as if it was an Easter egg hunt, but he kept cautioning them to slow down and get them all. He appeared to be about my age and height, but that was where the resemblance ended. I knew who he was right from the start. I remember thinking that if he lived in my neighbourhood and rode a bicycle it would be one that had the then fashionable wing handlebars that came up to either side of the rider. I was disdainful of them; they cut down on speed and manoeuverability. In fact they were only good for draping a satchel over to deliver papers. Still, they were all the rage. I knew, too, that he would have the back and front fenders removed and he would have moved one of his brake handles down to his crossbar. He was one of those who, if he was not appointed captain, was the first one picked.

Slung over his shoulder was one of the canvas bags that paper boys have. The lettering on it was indecipherable, and it seemed large for him, banging around his thighs as if he were wearing his father's trousers to a Hallowe'en party. Its strap had been shortened by knotting it at the top, but this only made it seem as if he had an epaulette on one shoulder. When he noticed Grandfather and me standing in the way, he seemed momentarily unsettled, as if we had managed to sneak up on him. He straightened up and with a practised shrug settled the strap of the satchel higher up on to his shoulder. He did this in the way I would imagine a guns-linger would resettle his holster on his hip; he did it absurdly well. The other two boys came up beside and slightly behind him, as if in formation.

This was the last sort of person I wanted to meet, and to make matters worse, my grandfather immediately began to confirm my suspicions about his inability to make the right introduction.

"Well, gents. Let me introduce my grandson Jonathan W. Corning. He is from the big city and the W. stands for Wildman. I guess you'll all be good friends. Jonathan, this is Wayne, Raymond and Patrick." It was not the right introduction, but Raymond and Patrick said hello. Wayne, the boy with the satchel, simply nodded. Then Raymond, apparently unaware of his reputation as one of the infamous Hueffer boys, actually made a friendly gesture.

"We're collectin' them. You wanna help?" He held his jar, half filled with beetles, directly up in front of my face. True to form, even in a crawling, heaving mass they remained strangely attractive; shining and continually moving as they were, it was something like looking into the glowing embers of a campfire. I managed to suppress a shudder, but before I could invent something appropriately enthusiastic to say, my grandfather spoke again.

"I can see you are concerned about the little fellows' welfare out here on the street, but cheek to jowl in a glass jar can't be all that comfortable either. Provided they have cheeks and jowls." His wit was lost upon us. Wayne shrugged his satchel up on his shoulder again and spoke.

"No, sir. We're just gonna burn 'em."

Grandfather ignored him completely. "Let's see, could be you'll take them to school and let them out in the cloakroom."

"No, sir. School's out. We're gonna..." Grandfather interrupted him before I could be sure if I heard a tinge of disdain in his voice.

"Maybe Sunday School then. I seem to recall that the good Reverend's sermons tend to crawl along."

"We're gonna pour gasoline on 'em."

"Or string them as necklaces or cover them with chocolate. By the look of the one I stepped on, they would be mint cream." I had heard my grandfather dig his heels in before and I was desperately trying to think of some way to change the topic. However, Wayne was stubborn too, and he simply went straight on.

"And then we'll burn 'em."

"Admirable. Train them to walk into the furnace and you have a sure fire thing. I can see the advertisement now.

'Throw those coal shovels away, buy a bunch of black beetles today.' Problem is, are they combustible? If you're gonna go into business you got to know these things if you're gonna make her go."

Blithely ignorant of the undertone of the conversation, Raymond Hueffer joined in. "They kind of curl up and smell bad, but they burn okay."

"Well, you see Wayne, that might be a problem right there. Coal doesn't smell so good, but people are used to it. Could be you got a crimp in your sales right there. Businessman has got to think these things through or he will get himself in trouble."

"We're not gonna do anything but burn 'em. My father said the more we got rid of the better it is. We pour gas on them and burn 'em." There was an unmistakable edge in Wayne's voice.

"Where are you getting the gasoline, Wayne?" The same sharpness was in Grandfather's voice.

"My father is George Maclenan and he owns the hardware store. We take it from the pump. He said we could."

"I know who your father is, and if he wants to run his business that way it's fine with me. But I don't want to see any fires near my end of town. If George Maclenan thinks it's such a good idea, he can have his beetle barbeque in front of the hardware store. From what I hear, he could use some excitement down there." He seemed about to say more, but then he turned to me. "Jonathan, you be back by one." He turned, and stepping carefully to avoid the beetles, he walked back the way we had come.

There was something in the tone of his voice that was unfair; he had somehow transgressed the rules between adults and children, and I think we all knew it. We were all simply standing there, watching him walk away when Wayne Maclenan broke the rules as well.

"My father says that if he had run his business as good as he talks, he would have been a rich man." I believe he intended his voice to carry to my grandfather; and it did.

We Renew Our Vows

The very first question that Raymond asked me after we turned away from my grandfather contained the clue to why I was not dismissed right away. They were interested in me, or at least Patrick and Raymond were, and Wayne, good general that he was, knew when to delay his attack.

"You live in the city."

I was not quite sure how to answer, so I settled for a nod.

Patrick continued the conversation. "My cousin lives in the city. We visit every Christmas."

Wayne ventured a comment. "Yeah, my father says it's a good place to visit but he wouldn't want to live there."

The nod seemed to work before, so I tried it again. Wayne was not satisfied, however, so he tried another tactic.

"Your grandfather is a weird old bird. My father says he talks more than he thinks. He's just an old woman." He was quite fond of quoting his father.

I relaxed immediately. Wayne had just ventured into one of my areas of expertise. My reply came almost automatically. "He's not a weird bird." I gave it a two-beat pause, more out of instinct than art. "He's an old parrot. No matter what you say to him he always answers back."

All Wayne could manage in reply was, "That's for sure." I had disarmed him, but I knew it was only momentary. Patrick and Raymond apparently considered my remark at least mildly humourous for they echoed Wayne's statement with considerable enthusiasm, laughter and in Raymond's case, an impromptu rendition of some sort of bird walk. Wayne was quick to bring it all back to business.

"Cut it out you guys. Let's get back to what we were doing. We got a block and a half to go. Jonathan, you can help if you want to. Use Raymond's jar. Wait till you see how many we got. Before we're through the whole street will be clean."

And so I spent one and a half hours collecting beetles. Held too closely, I feared their mint cream insides would escape all over my hands. Held too loosely and they would get turned around, their legs beating minor tattoos on my palm. The worst was when they finally sensed you were going to capture them and they would scurry off. I kept imagining that if I grasped quickly, I might miscalculate with the obvious result. Still, I would have happily done it all day, perhaps even all summer. My earlier experience with co-operation in the storming of the hockey boards had shown me the delight of planned and co-operative effort. That day, collecting beetles showed me the safety of such an enterprise.

It was, I suppose, a matter of having a script. We all knew our parts. It was safe. I was happy to speak my lines and they gave a kind of shape to my day, which otherwise had been seriously deteriorating. Granted, the veneer was thin. Whenever I glanced behind me I could see at least one beetle who had been overlooked, but I was not going to point out the inherent weaknesses in the scheme. I knew where that would get me, and I was determined to fit in. If there had been a worksong I would have sung right along. Lift that Beetle, Tote that Jar.

The town was basically a simple cross form. Main Street went East and West, and Centre Street went North and South. Most of the business establishments were on Main Street, but a few dribbled up for a block either way on Centre. Our plan was to work up Centre, past Barstow's shop finish off near the curling-rink. Wayne kept exhorting us to be thorough and encouraging us with how close we were to completion. My only hope was that we would not have to go

83

back the way we came, because I was sure even the most ardent adherence to the fiction that we were making progress would be shaken by seeing the many beetles who had wandered onto the sidewalk after our passing. Fortunately, when we were done, we went to the curling-rink.

The curling-rink was a huge half-cylinder of corrugated tin. Although there were very low walls before the arc of the roof began, it seemed to rest upon the ground like a giant upside-down eavestrough. Standing beside the lot where Fowler's Equipment left the trade-in machinery, and in the midst of the ramshackle sheds and out-buildings behind Main Street, it was impressively bright. We went in through a small access door from the pumphouse at the back; inside was impressively dim. Raymond Hueffer actually had to guide me to a bench while my eyes became accustomed to the light.

With a metal roof, the building interior should have been hot, but it was not. Nor was it cool. Instead, the change that I felt was from activity to stillness. We were sitting on bleachers. Arranged on a wooden rail in front of me were perhaps fifteen quart mason jars filled with beetles. It was too dim to be horrified at what was going on in the jars (or what was not going on in the jars), but there was enough light that looking past them I could see the wooden outlines of three curling-rinks spreading out before me. Where the ice would have been in the winter was pebbled with gravel. Light came in from four small dusty windows behind me. It also starred from tiny holes in the roof; they may have been rivet holes or nail holes, but at evenly spaced intervals down the length of the building were arcs of irregularly spaced points of light.

It was the perfect place—indeed the inevitable place—to end a hard day of beetle collecting. It was not the place for the elaborate purpose that had been occupying us, but that occupation was over. It had the kind of nostalgia that clings to empty school gymnasiums, empty churches and empty stages; it compelled lowered tones of voice so that every statement took on the air of confidence. It was a place of imagination; it was the neighbourhood garage on a rainy day; it was the rink shack in the summer; in fact, in a curious way, it was like the hockey-rink boards earlier that spring.

Raymond spoke first. "Pretty nice, eh?"

"Yeah, this is just great." My expression of enthusiasm needed work, but I was trying.

Wayne, however, delivered his line with exactly the right amount of casualness. "Care for a smoke?"

I was not a more honest child than any other, and I did not particularly value honesty, but I think it is fair to say that even as far back as my early experiences in the playground I had maintained a certain integrity. It had been easy enough to play along with the collection of beetles, and even my earlier condemnation of Grandfather as a parrot had not bothered me; I owed him no allegiance whatsoever.

"Sure. Got any cigars?"

I could tell Patrick was impressed by the tone of his voice. "You smoke cigars?"

"Only when I can get them."

Raymond was impressed as well. "We just collect the butts and roll them up. We've never had a real smoke. You get good cigar butts down in front of the hotel on Sunday morning. Sometimes they throw them away Saturday night even before they are half done."

As Wayne spoke he was reaching down under the bench. "Give him your life's story, Hueffer, it will probably only take a minute. Here, Corning, you can smoke this."

The cigar he gave me was less than a third gone. As nearly as possible, I followed my grandfather's actions in lighting it, but still I waited for a taunting voice to say, "Sure you smoke, Corning." No-one said anything. Furthermore, I knew what was to happen to boys who smoked their first cigar. In the stories I read they became green and nauseated.

85

I did not. In fact, I suddenly felt a great relaxation. I almost laughed out loud when Wayne spoke again.

"You better knock that ash off in the gravel. Somebody could see it in the bleachers, and that would be just too bad."

I took the cigar out of my mouth and looked at it with great regret. "Oh, sure, I can do that. You know, the long ash filters the air. It cools the smoke. At least that's what I've found."

It worked and it worked perfectly. Patrick and Raymond started to pay me the kind of court they had been paying to Wayne; Wayne could do nothing. For my part, I could do nothing wrong. I inadvertently created a smoke ring and it lifted out in front of us, cross-sectioned into secret whorls by a descending shaft of light. After an impossibly bad beginning, I had come through beautifully. Unlike earlier in the spring, there was no sitting off to one side. I played the game, and I played it well. It was a less innocent feeling of elation than I had experienced after conquering the hockey-rink boards, but it was more powerful. Raymond and Patrick began listing off the town's attractions for my approval; there was the swimming hole on the Sortie River, the café on Friday night, a place where you could look into the Dance Hall, Bertram Hueffer's '49 Dodge pickup truck with the special back wheels, Mrs. Roget's pension-day visit to the Ladies and Escorts and her subsequent pension-night ejection from the same establishment, and the list continued. I listened graciously to it all, staring at my cigar judiciously and making appropriately interested remarks at the right time.

Then the mermaid appeared.

Patrick was speaking. "Yeah, when Wayne says it's okay, we go out to the bandstand and watch his sister dance. She's only thirteen, but she's got it all."

There is little excuse for what happened next. And now I feel strangely guilty about it or perhaps unworthy in some way, as if I had somehow transgressed a basic integrity. My grandfather would have said that I muddied the water. Still it was so simple to do: I threw the mermaid to the wolves. In doing so, I sometimes wonder if I lost her for good. I know that as I described my experience with her, the fence I had climbed became higher, the risks I had taken became greater, and even now I can remember how I ended it. Borrowing Michael's phrase from the playground that spring, I stretched my arms out in front of my chest as far as they would go, and cupping my hands in front of me, I said, "She's got them. Right out to there."

My victory, if that is an appropriate word, was complete. Raymond and Patrick were entranced. Any attempt by Wayne, I thought, to top my story or expose me was defeated forever. Perhaps I sensed his enmity would be equally long lasting, but I did not worry about it. I was invulnerable.

Forever, as it turned out, was terminated by the arrival of Bobby Scott.

I now find it impossible to remember what I first thought of Bobby that day in the curling-rink. The layers of later words have settled over him like the dust that settled over the town that spring, but instead of preserving him, he seems almost obscured. There are a few things about him that might be counted upon as fact. He had been a blue baby, which confused me considerably when I was younger. His father had left Union and he and his mother played a role in town somewhere between charity and condemnation. His nicknames were Blue Boy, Normal Bob, Rubber Boy and The Wriggler. These last two names were the result of his mild inability to control certain body movements which was, I realize now, probably a result of oxygen deprivation at birth. At times all of his physical responses seemed to be exaggerated; a small chuckle in anyone else was a storm of laughter in Bobby that waved him back and forth like a current waves seaweed; a momentary surprise not only widened his eyes, but it would drop his jaw and bring his fingers fumbling up to his mouth. He was a year older than me, but he was smaller and more frail. But these few facts aside, it seems almost impossible to fix a steady picture of him in my memory. The roles assigned to him by the town were so pervasive that it was hard at first to see him clearly. He was, of course, the ideal victim, and that fact was apparent on the very first meeting.

Bobby announced his arrival by falling down. I was shocked by the sudden noise, but the other three boys simply laughed. When we were introduced, he smiled and ducked his head to one side. I thought he was just another in a rather typical line of scapegoats, not unlike Biggs.

The quietness that Wayne had been nursing broke into words when Bobby sat down.

"Well, here's something you don't have in the city." He paused. "Hey, Rubber Boy, sit still for Corning so he can have a good look at you."

Bobby smiled, giggled slightly, but he was caught in some current and could not sit still.

"C'mon, Rubber Boy. Sit still."

"Aw, Wayne, I can't. You know."

"Sure you can. Try real hard for me, Wormy."

As Bobby attempted to be still, he waved harder.

"You couldn't sit still if your life depended on it could you?"

"Naw, I couldn't."

Patrick and Raymond broke into laughter and Bobby obligingly giggled. The three boys spoke in a practised chorus.

"Some people call him Normal Bob."

"Some people call him Rubber Boy."

"Some people say he's one brick short."

"Some people say he's half a load."

"Some people say he broke his lead."

"Some people say he lost his eraser."

It seemed like the right place for me to contribute.

"And that's why they call him Rubber Boy."

It was not particularly subtle, but it elicited great laughter from Raymond and Patrick. Bobby vibrated quite happily over it, and the baiting seemed about to pass away. But Wayne would not let it go.

"Some people say he is just a Retard and should be put in a home."

Bobby's smile got wider and his continual movement almost became like an exaggerated nod, but there was a frightened confusion in his eyes.

"No. Naw. You shouldn't say that Wayne." He reached into his pocket and carefully took something out. Holding it cupped in his hands, he looked at it while the negative shake of his head gradually subsided.

"Watcha got there?"

"I found him this morning, Wayne. I named him Clack because my mother said he sounded like that."

Wayne reached over and quickly plucked the beetle from Bobby's hand.

"Aw, Wayne, don't put him in the jar. Please. He's mine."

Wayne turned back from the railing and held up two closed fists in front of him.

"Which hand?"

"Don't squeeze, Wayne. Don't squeeze." Bobby sat at the edge of the bench, his hands clasped between his legs, alternately raising and lowering each foot. He was in an agony of indecision, looking first at one hand and then at the other.

"You better choose. I'm thinking about starting to squeeze."

In the dim light Bobby seemed to shrink and expand with each breath.

"Which hand?"

Bobby was biting his knuckles. Even from where I was I could see the indentations on his skin. I spoke out.

"The left hand."

"Is that the one?"

Bobby moved up and down rapidly. Wayne opened his hand slowly and Bobby carefully cupped up the beetle. Once again, as he held it he seemed to subside. Slowly Wayne opened his right hand.

"I think you got the wrong one Wormy, I think this one is Clack." Wayne pretended to examine the beetle in his right hand closely. "Yep. This one is Clack all right."

Both beetles were the same, but Bobby was convinced. He set the beetle he was holding down on the railing and stood up facing Wayne. It was as if he knew what was going to happen.

"I guess if I do something for you like giving back old Clack here, you would be willing to do something for me."

Bobby moved up and down. "Sure, Wayne, I'll do something."

"Would you walk the railway trestle?"

Bobby nodded.

"Would you call Mr. Domanski a dumb Polack?"

"Sure, Wayne. I'd do that."

"Let the air out of old Elliot's tires?"

"I'll do it. Sure."

"Then I guess what you better do is come along and get us some ice from behind the hotel."

Bobby kept on smiling, but first his head and then his whole upper body began to move from side to side.

"I don't fit up there anymore. I grew since last year. It's marked on the kitchen door. I grew Wayne."

"C'mon Rubber Boy, you didn't grow. Just slink up the chute like last year and trip the catch."

Raymond Hueffer spoke. "Jeez, Wayne. If he gets caught again he could be in real trouble. I heard my father saying..."

"Who gives a damn what your father says, Hueffer. He won't get caught. If you're worried, maybe you could get us some ice." Wayne closed his fist on the beetle, brought it up to his ear and shook it like he was rolling dice. "What do you say, Rubber Boy? Clack is starting to rattle."

Bobby did not say yes, but his body spoke for him. He seemed to become smaller and more frail.

The ice machine was located behind the Union Hotel. When I saw the size of the ice chute I thought there would be no chance that Bobby could even get part way in. I could tell that Patrick and Raymond were nervous. Raymond actually tried to deflect the situation again. "Jeez, Wayne. I think he has grown. If he gets caught up there again, he's in big trouble."

I tried to help. "Yeah, well I don't see what we need ice for anyways."

"What you think, Hueffer, doesn't matter, and as far as I'm concerned, Corning, if you're scared, then run home to Grandpa and let him talk your ear off. Both of you should button up. If I say he's not going to have trouble, then he's not going to have any trouble. C'mon Blue Boy, in you go. I'll put Clack right here on the curb. He's in the sun and he won't move. Do it."

The situation had suddenly become completely inevitable, and Bobby was the first to recognize it. He went down on his knees in front of the chute. He seemed to stop and think for a moment. I fully expected everyone to see the impossibility of his fitting into the chute when, without further ado, putting one arm and shoulder in first, he somehow turned and placed his head inside as well. He paused for a moment and then began half scrambling, half undulating up the chute. When he had disappeared to his waist he stopped, one hand still out, pressed closely to his crotch. He had turned over on his back so that he seemed like a mechanic under a car, one hand out waiting for a wrench. Suddenly his hand started flipping rapidly as if all the movement he normally enjoyed had to be compensated for by four fingers and a thumb. It was apparent to all of us that he was going to get stuck and that, in fact, he must barely have room to breathe. Wayne leaned down and spoke up the chute.

"C'mon Bobby. Quit fooling around. Either go up or come down.

Bobby must have made some sound because Wayne leaned his head up against the freezer. The words "Party Time," written as if in some musical script, floated like a banner on the freezer just above his head.

There was no answering sound. "C'mon Bobby. I'm not kidding. Get out of there or I'll squash that stupid Clack flat as a pancake."

This time we all heard Bobby. It was just as if he were breathing fast and each breath was expired with a muffled scream. Suddenly, his feet started to kick and almost flutter like he was swimming underwater. Then he stopped.

"Jeez. Pull him out, Wayne." Raymond Hueffer knelt down and both of them took a leg and pulled as hard as they could. I saw that Patrick was already backing away, watching intently, one hand to the fence as if feeling his way in the darkness. The steady muffled screaming started again.

"Oh, Jeez, Wayne. He is really stuck. I'm getting out of here." Raymond Hueffer stood up, took one look at me and then turned and took flight. We heard a window bang open in the hotel and a woman's voice.

"What are you kids... Oh, my God."

Wayne turned to me. "That's his old lady. She and old Houghton will be coming. It was his idea. That's the story. It was his idea, and if you say any different, you'll be sorry." He turned and ran in the same direction as Raymond.

I knelt down, caught his kicking ankles and tried to talk to him. I had heard somewhere that when they hanged criminals they kicked their feet. "Bobby, Bobby, I'm here. Just relax. Someone's coming. Just relax."

I kept talking to him while Mr. Houghton and Bobby's mother unlocked the top of the freezer and stacked blocks of ice in the dust off to the side. They made little rivulets of black mud. I kept talking. When they finally got the front unhinged and pulled it away, Mrs. Scott was crying quietly.

I think I expected Bobby to be dead. He was not. He was, however, slightly blue, a fact that now strikes me as ironic. His mother chafed his wrists, then his shoulders. Mr. Houghton packed the layers of ice back into the freezer. He left the bottom layer melting in the dust. He turned and spoke to me.

"Who are you?"

I told him.

"Was this your idea?"

"No, sir."

"Was it his idea?" He seemed incredulous.

"No, sir."

"Whose was it?"

I could tell that Mr. Houghton was very angry. I was very tired. In fact, I was as weary as I could ever remember being.

"It was Wayne's idea. Wayne Maclenan."

"There will be more said about this. Jennifer, you're gonna have to do something with him sooner or later. This is not working out."

Jennifer did not look up at him.

"Thank you, Jim. We'll be all right now."

I stood and watched. She made him stand up on his feet. It looked like he had been drooling, although it could have been the ice. Then, half carrying him, she started toward the street. She stopped and looked around at me.

"God bless you for staying with him. You're a good person to do that. I'll tell your grandfather so, too. My son always listens to the wrong boys. I'm going to tell him to listen to you."

I was left with the summer crumbling around my ears. Actually, it would probably be more accurate to say it was crumbling before my eyes. The town unravelled before me. It was as if the stumbling passage of Mrs. Scott and Bobby had somehow unzipped the town behind them so that I saw it as it really was for the first time. It was like one of those illustrations for children, "How Many Animals Can You See in This Picture?" You look, and finding one you suddenly see dozens more. Only with me, it was not animals; I admitted to myself I did not want to spend the summer in Union; I saw that I had started the summer in a kind of open warfare with Wayne Maclenan and his friends; I accepted that Union was not going to protect me from all the things I wanted protection from. The roses in glass, the globe of the world, the walnuts, the peppermints, all of them were simply what they seemed to be.

And as suddenly as I admitted all of the things that I had been trying to deny, it was as if some glue that had been holding the town together dissolved, and everything altered before my eyes.

For a moment, I was looking at the dingy collection of buildings, dust covered, some of them sagging, angles askew. Then they even ceased to be buildings and became merely planes, angles and surfaces that were connected only by virtue of lining the same street. I saw the broad slash of rust that had dribbled from the wire mesh that covered the movie poster at the Lux, and seeing it there for the first time, it was as if it had just then bled over the picture and the words. I noticed for the first time that Elliot's General Store had a rectangle of new wood where a window had been boarded in, and suddenly the whole surface seemed like a patchwork, barely stitched together and unrecognizable as a wall. I noticed that the sign on the wall had been painted over an old sign but slightly off centre so that both seemed to be sinking into the wood even as I looked.

I backed into the board fence that ran behind the hotel. It was used for posting bills and notices and posters of upcoming events. Fragments of messages momentarily asserted themselves: Estate Sale, 5 May; Loden's Auction, Rural Route Six, West of the Bridge; Dance! Dance!; Rummage

Sale; Bake Sale. As soon as each message became clear, it would fade. I stepped back and saw that no poster was ever taken down. New notices were simply pasted over the old, so that there was layer after layer after layer of indecipherable print and faded paper lifting tattered corners and shredding and blurring in the weather. The whole fence was like sunburned and peeling skin. I stepped further back and it changed once more. The sun shining through the vertically fastened boards of the fence had faded regular white lines on the peeling paper making it half a grid on some unreadable map. Stepping back once more, simply trying to make sense of it, I felt the briefest resistance beneath my heel and then heard and felt a faint sound like the crinkling of a cellophane wrapper. I knew without looking that I had stepped back on Bobby's beetle. Without looking down, I scraped my shoe on the boardwalk and began running toward my grandparent's house. Although it might seem melodramatic, I should also add that I stumbled as I ran.

When I arrived back at the house, I stopped at the front gate. Grandfather was there, standing at the verandah as I had seen him stand a hundred times before, his hands on the railing and looking like the captain of some musical comedy stage ship. Although he seemed to be staring straight into the distance, he noticed me.

"Well Jonathan. You're a bit late. You've been hatching plots with your new business associates, I guess." Although I do not believe that I was showing any evidence of how upset I was, I was so absurdly grateful that at least he was remaining the same that the relief must have shown. By the time I reached the door, he spoke again.

"I guess maybe you walked into the combine today. Maybe you better come over here and sit down for a while. It's been my experience that a verandah always helps a man to think." I could hear the quietness in his voice. I had never heard it there before, but just then I did not care. I simply

95

wanted whatever he was going to say to be over. I wanted the day to be over, and for that matter, the summer. I would have left right then except for the chair that I was sitting on. I realize now that it was the first time I had ever sat there. In fact, I had never even wanted to sit there; it had not seemed special to me. But it was.

Grandfather's chair was a simple spindle-backed affair; it was also one of the most comfortable chairs I had ever sat in. Indeed, I have probably not sat in its like since. Although each piece of wood in the chair was as hard and unyielding as wood ever is, each spindle and even the seat of the chair were only joined loosely with the rest, and so while it was not soft, it formed itself to me. It was just another one of the endless surprises of the afternoon, but this one did not frighten me. Instead, I began to examine the chair closely and almost with wonder. First I twisted round and looked at the dowels that formed the back of the chair, and even today I can scarcely believe I had never before noticed what I then saw. Small bits of bright wool, snippets of string, shreds of fabric tipped out from each of the dowel joints where the spindles went into the top piece, and it was the same where they went into the bottom. Holding onto the seat, I craned over and saw that where the leg braces met the legs had been neatly wrapped with binder twine. I reached down and touched it. The twine had been rubbed and worn as smooth as silk. Almost every one of the joints of the chair had been doctored, and some of the bits of wool were newer and some older so that the logic of it was clear. As each joint had lost its glue and given way, he had taken whatever was on hand to bolster it up. I suddenly felt as if we shared a secret. I looked up to where he was standing to see if he knew.

He was looking away and straight out toward the east. He began to speak. "Guess you kind of got caught in the combine today. I guess that's my fault. It's gotta be somebody's fault. Things usually are. Somebody is usually to blame. I was kicked out of the Hardware by Wayne Maclenan's father. Said I talked too much. How can someone talk so much that a man will ask for silence? How can that be? How can anybody talk that much? My stories are bullshit he says. Bullshit! Gawddamn. How can a man's life be bullshit? Sure I shine them up a bit, polish them a bit. But bullshit? My gawd, how can he use those words? I've been standing here trying to figure it out and it just comes back to the fact that some child can call lines at me on the street. That's what it comes to. By gawd, his kid must've learned it from him. But right there on the street?"

There was a regret in his voice so intense it was confusion. He was still standing stock-still looking out past the grain elevators. I think that for the first time in his life he did not care if anyone at all was listening. And hearing that undirected intensity of voice, I saw that I was facing the final and worst change of the day. So while he from his side had given up on listeners, I from my side lowered my head, looked down at the chair and tried not to listen at all. But I heard him.

"Yessir. You can see a long way from up here. I can see Cumberland County. Northumberland Strait. Way off there between the grain elevators just like a rifle sight. Over 50 years ago. He was a quiet man, but he was fair too. Slow of speech. 'You can have a man's say, Roderick, when you do a man's work. Until then you will do what you are told.' How many times did he say that? Me and my brother John did a man's work. Red dirt. We used to plough the herring in. People won't believe that, I suppose. Me and John would sometimes take enough in one net for the whole boat. He'd say, 'C'mon you shiny fellows, let's go swimming in the spuds.' And we'd spread those sons of bitches on the red dirt and then plough them in. But now it's just bullshit. Just old man Caldwell's bullshit. By gawd, how the gulls would squeal and squawk over that bullshit. Guess they must have thought they were fish. Guess they hadn't heard about me... And father would stand there behind that plough like a captain on a ship."

He stopped for a moment. I looked up. He was not so much staring out as he was listening. I found myself straining to hear as well.

"Me and John heard about it down Frenchman's Road. Bunch of fellows talking. Me and John stood back and listened. Gawddamn I loved it even then! It was just the usual talk, quiet in the evening, but some fellow from Montreal started to get windy about women. In Montreal they swam up the street like spawning salmon is what he said. We just sat back listening. We were young, not too close up to the step.

"Then somewhere in all the talk of women we heard it. Spurlines! Spurlines into new country. She's good good farmland, he said. Free as a Montreal woman, he said, and we all laughed. Gawd, I was young. But then we'd heard. Yessir, we had heard. We held onto those words like plough handles. By gawd, it was bullshit that built this country. It was men talking behind the mill who built her. Not silence- ...not silence."

Then he was silent, and it was frightening. I held onto the seat of the spindle-backed chair as if the verandah was going to break loose and spin away.

"Oh there was silence, too. But my brother John had all the words you'd ever want. All that fall we thought about it. Those fall storms, me in my bed and him in his. Wave would wash. He'd say, 'We go this spring, Rod.' Wave'd wash. 'I'll tell father after Christmas.' Wave'd wash. 'West in the spring... Could be that we'll marry. You'll take one grant... And I will too... We'll plough our own land... Let someone else plough the fish.' Seems now like all that winter I went to sleep with the waves and his voice. Gawddamn he had a way with words. What would he say today? 'If you can't talk, you can't sing. If you can't sing, you can't dance. And if you can't dance, Rod, then you're no brother of mine.' He'd take this gawddamn Maclenan silence and

98

break it into 50 pieces. By gawd, he would."

He was holding onto the railing of the verandah, pulling it toward him and pushing it away. It seemed like it would break.

"No, sir. It was not the government that made this country. It wasn't work. It wasn't greed. It wasn't some gawddamned life-sized statue of the pioneer. It was words! It wasn't even the railroad that took us out here. It was John talking. Jesus, some of those people didn't even know English, but John could talk to them. He'd stamp his feet, slap his thigh and laugh and sing, and by gawd, they understood and talked back the same way. They understood. We understood. We were all going the same place. We were all talking about the same thing. Words took us out here and it was words again when we got here. Me and John and Queen Victoria and the Dominion of Canada and I still have the paper."

He began fumbling, looking for something in his pockets and then he became still, slowly lowering his hands back to his sides.

"Even before we signed we took her with words. We stood on the hill behind where the house would be. It looked good to me, but I wasn't sure. I closed my eyes and tried to remember all we talked about back home. Then I opened them and looked out. It wasn't what I'd dreamed of. It wasn't what I'd seen when John talked away back home. It was so gawddamned big and the sky so deep and wide you could fall into it and drown. It was like waking up from sleep and not knowing who you are or what day it is. I closed my eyes again and just listened. Wind. That's all I heard. Wind. It'd been 3000 miles and all I could hear was wind brushing up through the long grass. That's all I could smell. Then I could taste it. Rain far off. I waited and it blew all my words away into that gawddamned sky and I knew I was lost, but I couldn't say it. I knew there had to be some words or I'd never get back!"

99

And sitting on my chair, I was lost too and had no words to speak. I held my breath and waited, and waited, and finally heard him take a deep, deep breath.

"He said, 'This is it, Rod', and it was like John's words called me back. 'This is It. This is where we stick the pry bar in. Chop a hole in the boat, brother. This is where we stay. Look at her. Look at her, Rod! She's free and she's fresh and others may have passed over but she's gonna be ours. We'll spread no stinking herring here.' By gawd, he reached down and pulled up a clump of that wool like his hand was a shovel. 'Smell her, Rod. You smell any fish? She's sweeter than roses.' He was laughing and jumping around. 'Listen to her, Rod, listen to her talk. We'll find out what she wants and we'll give it to her.' He hit me on the side of the head with that clod and knocked me ass over heels. I looked up at him and he was leaping around. 'We'll find out what she needs and we'll steal it if we have to.' And he laughed and danced, and he had all the words, and there was no silence to get lost in when he was there. He let you know who you were and where you were and he put up with no gawddamned silence. How he danced that day. I just lay there and watched."

Grandfather was moving back and forth at the railing, slow deliberate steps. He seemed caged in, but I think I worried that in some way he was going to escape and leave me alone. Finally, he spoke again.

"We hired out to old Carson. Built the first barn on our time. Slept in the loft. Long about October it was colder than we ever knew. Every morning before the sun, by gawd before the stove, he'd warm it up. Stamp his feet, look up to where the house was gonna be and laugh. Then he'd sing. 'It's cold by gawd. It's cold by gawd. It's cold by gawd in the barn. But it's better by far, but it's better by far, but it's better by far than the house.' And I'd look at that blue cold snow where we planned the house and it was too cold to think, but I'd have to laugh and I'd start to move. Silence?

Silence would have froze us to death."

He seemed like a horse stamping with flies, shaking, tail swishing, about to run once more down the fence line in an attempt to escape their bites.

"My brother, John, said, 'Well, Rod, Old Man Carson talked about logging on the coast. I reckon we'll freeze for wages.' Oh, yes. That's what he said. I am not talking bullshit now, Maclenan. Gawd, how I wish I was. Word had come. Good money for loggers. Yessir, the Word had come. By the end of October we were on the Island and four days later we were in the camp. Money to prove up the grants in the spring. I listened to him from sea to gawd-damned sea and not once did I ask him for silence. Not once did I want it.

"Lice. Rubbed raw. Hands too cold to untangle the traces. Calluses on calluses on calluses. Food stinks worse than dead cow in mid-summer. But no worse than us. It was February. No, March. We had enough and there was talk. They weren't even going to give us our bedrolls. How do you find words for that? But John did. He talked to Davis. We had to prove up the homestead. We had to make good on that piece of paper. We figured two days' walk. 'Two days, Rod,' he said, 'Two days, a hot bath, smoking cigars and counting our money.'

"It snowed the first night. And it didn't pack, and it didn't blow. It just snowed and snowed and snowed. Thigh deep and all day for ten miles. Oh, Christ, Maclenan wants silence. Why doesn't he go walk in the snow. 'Trade off on the lead boys, trade off on the lead.' And John kept talking. He roped us together with his voice. Made each man say who he was, where from, where to. Tied us together but it started to fray. 'We do her together boys or we go down one by one. Sing out if you start to fade.' Morning of the third day. It was the young Swede who was first. Went down and John sat him up and talked to him. He just looked off the way a dog does or a horse when he's going. Didn't speak a word of English but John talked to him for two hours. Two gawddamned hours. Tried to put his eyes back in his head. The others left. I'd never see John scared before. Sitting on his heels in front of that poor Swede. He didn't look even sixteen. After a while, John just stared at him, sat on his heels and just stared like he was trying to out-wait him. John stared at the Swede and the Swede stared off.

"Gawddamn, I was scared. Strangest gawddamned thing, I was scared cold. I got cold inside. Get up John. I knew it had to be me. Fire in the barn, John. The old man coming up the stairs with the strap, John. Hop to it. Train's off the track, John. Let's get her back on. I said every fool thing that came into my head. I got him up and following me but he wouldn't say a thing. I used every word I had. I told every lie. I said every story. I spoke every secret. Everything I'd ever wanted. Everything I'd ever feared. But he wouldn't speak back. I remembered poems clear back to father's knee.

"*Oh come all ye landsmen and listen to me. Bide away from your tasks for a while.* Remember it John? We used to do it together. *I will tell you a tale of the salt-laden sea and the murderous crocodile.* You do one verse and I'll do one. Remember that bend? And that deadfall? Slide. Shove John. My wrists are cold, John. Gawddamn it they ache. How did that poem go John? You could always remember poems. How did it go? *I travelled down him full a month or more till I came to his leathery craw.* What was next? Can't you remember? *There I met with rum kegs that rolled on the floor and plenty of beef and straw.* Remember it? What's that sound? We can make it John. We gotta keep pushing. We gotta keep pressing on."

He seemed to be talking to me. He kept glancing back at me as he spoke. I tried desperately to think of something to say to him, but before I could answer another wild question would spill out.

"John, can you hear it? Listen. Harness bells. Oh sweet Jesus John, it's voices. We've made it. Can you hear the voices John? Tell me can you? John? John? JOHN?"

He was turned around and looking directly at me.

"For Christ's sake, answer."

He was looking straight through me.

"John?"

We were both silent, waiting for some answer. He shook his head, flicking the invisible fly.

"Oh, gawddamn, oh, gawddamn, oh, gawddamn, oh, gawddamn."

It was almost a song the way he said it.

"He was eight miles back. I'd been talking to no-one. No-one had been listening. I'd been talking to silence and I had let it go, let it pass. They brought him in. I went out to look. Gawddamn he was so quiet. He was blue. It was the strangest colour. It wasn't sky blue, and it wasn't sea blue. It wasn't robin's egg blue. It wasn't... It was silent blue. Like no other blue I'd ever seen."

His breath was coming unevenly making his voice ragged.

"They asked me what words I wanted said over him. I said I'd do it. I just told him laying there that I'd learn how to do all that he said. I'd speak the words. I told him I'd do all the talking from then on. Because I knew then, I'd had enough of silence. I had enough silence to last me a lifetime. When I got back here I talked. Talked to the horses when I ploughed. And I talked to the dirt. I talked to the weather. Because that's what he would have done. If you can't talk, you can't sing. If you can't sing, you can't dance. If you can't dance, you're gonna die!

"We went all the way, me and Ruby. House, farm, children, but the silence started to grow. Kids left. Silence came back, just like it had been waiting. I came in, built the store. Thought of Bellam but went for Union and she's not going anywhere, John. I thought for a while that the store would do it. You were right. She was young and she was pretty but I must have said the wrong things because she's gone away. And all I've got is silence. What do you say,

John? What do I do now?"

I knew he was not talking to me, and I knew as clearly that I had to say something. I was crying. I was listening and looking and searching for the right words. Suddenly, I had them. They did not seem like mine. I took a deep breath and spoke.

"Grandfather." He didn't hear me.

"Grandfather." He turned.

"Grandfather, the grapefruit tree. She looks pretty good, Grandfather. I think she could bloom this year."

He did not move. I looked away, afraid of what was going to happen. But I was listening as hard as he had listened. I cannot know what was on his mind, what he weighed and balanced, what he feared or hoped; I simply waited in the silence. Random sounds jumped out. A truck went over the board bridge at the north end of town making a sound like distant thunder. Crows battled somewhere across the street. I heard him moving toward me. I felt his hand on my shoulder. It felt like the spindles on the back of the chair, each finger hard and unyielding, but somehow comforting. I stood up. Half leaning on me, half guiding me, we made our way toward the grapefruit tree. He placed my hand upon the trunk.

"Is she real?"

"Yes."

"Is she real?"

"Yes."

"Sing it out. Is She Real?"

"Yes, Grandfather. She's real."

"You're gawddamned right she is, John, and I'm good for one more. We'll set the sons of bitches on their ears. We'll tell them what's been said. We'll make them dance, John. Yes, we will. We'll string them the tale of their gawd-damned lives."

Standing there once more, my hand on the bark of the tree, I remembered the echo from the first time. It seemed to me then a thousand years before.

We had renewed our vows.

We Set Forth

I rose late that following day. My grandmother had heard about my escapade at the ice machine because Bobby's mother had telephoned to commend my behaviour. Grandmother acknowledged my fortitude by letting me sleep late. I had breakfast alone and then went out to survey the morning from the verandah. The first thing I realized was that I was reluctant to sit in my grandfather's chair. It suddenly seemed like too great a familiarity. I felt fragile, as if the inside of me and the outside of me were separated by only the most insubstantial of membranes. As on the day before, the town seemed new, even raw. Only the grapefruit tree, its leaves a waxy, leathery green, seemed rooted. All the rest seemed as insubstantial as my ribcage felt. Grandfather walked around the corner of the house and up the stairs before he noticed me.

"Well Jonathan..." He paused. In our minds I think each of us heard him finish the statement in one of his typical ways: "Sun's on the move, I guess we better be too" or "Wise men and rich people are still in bed, now is our chance." But we both realized the old lines were no longer applicable, and he did not speak. He walked over and stood beside me looking out at the street. Finally, he simply said "Good Morning." I replied in kind. The silence we stood in was not companionable; it was awkward.

It seems to me now that I knew many things as I stood there. I knew that words travelled faster than anything but light, and that somewhere in town Wayne or one of his friends was exaggerating my role of informer to anyone who would listen; I knew I probably had been branded a sissy or even worse; and above all, I knew that Union would cast no spell over me that summer as I had hoped. On the previous day I had seen the town unravel before me, and I knew that to glue it back together again would be a formidable task.

Grandfather, too, was standing in the shadow of the previous day; the town had been unravelling for him, as well. It was as if we both had a story to tell, and we both realized we needed each other to listen to it. The silence was like a prelude to some sort of contract we had to forge. The grapefruit tree was as stubbornly green as it had been the day before, but I was not going to speak of it, regardless of the fact that it was our one certain bond. I knew that if I did and failed to say the right thing, whatever contract we were attempting would be lost forever.

I found myself watching two beetles as they clacked across the bars of shadow cast by the verandah railing. Whenever they moved over a shaded bar their direction was aimless, but when they reached a lighted space their path would straighten out until they reached the next bar of shadow. I remembered reading in a Mark Trail comic-strip that some insects orient themselves by sunlight. I knew that something had to be said, and I was stoically preparing to begin the day's negotiations by referring to them when, from out of nowhere, a voice spoke.

"Speak up." It was not my grandfather. He was as startled as I was. It was as if some deity had decided to admonish us.

"Go on now, speak up." Jennifer-Rose Scott was standing out on the sidewalk at the far corner of the yard. Beside her, standing on the lower rail of the fence, holding on to the pickets like some diminutive jailbird, was Robert Baker Scott, more commonly known as Rubber Boy, Mr. Normal, That Poor Scott Boy and other names too numerous to mention. Wavering faintly, as if still shivering from the ice machine, or perhaps shimmering in heat waves that were not yet apparent to anyone else, Bobby stared intently over the fence at us.

"Oh for goodness sakes Bobby, say hello to Jonathan and Mr. Caldwell." Grandfather and I were still speechless, and Bobby started leaning back from the fence and then pulling himself upward and forward, as if preparing himself for some sort of leap. His movement gave Grandfather the cue he needed to remember his lines, and he launched into them with vehemence.

"Better listen to the lady, stranger. A man stands on my picket fence like that and I start to feel like a tiger in a cage. You better speak your piece before I start to growl."

I often had trouble knowing when to take him seriously, but apparently Bobby did not. He began to smile, and his backward and forward motion increased proportionately until it seemed like he was standing on a swing and pumping it upwards like a trapeze artist trying to get the height for a triple somersault. His smiling face appeared and disappeared from behind the fence until he had developed enough momentum to take the leap.

"Good morning Mr. Caldwell. Good morning Jonathan. You have a good set of values." It was obvious that his mother had coached him about what to say, but the contrast between the formality of the words and the unorthodox delivery made the speech spontaneous. His mother was clearly pleased by his performance, and she smiled down at him with an intensity that matched his own. Grandfather, of course, could not let such an opportunity go by. He stepped to the railing in exaggerated surprise, and shading his eyes like a sailor looking for land, he peered out at the street. I felt the first tickling of embarrassment and irritation at his antics.

"By gawd, that is no stranger. That sounds like somebody I know." He looked over his shoulder and spoke to me directly for the first time that morning. "Jonathan, you figure we know this fellow? He sounds familiar. You figure he is friend or foe?"

"Aw Mr. Caldwell. It's me, Bobby Scott."

"By gawd Jonathan, I think it is. It's Robert Baker Scott back from the frozen North. Come up here and tell us about your travels, Bob. Jonathan, bring that man aboard."

As Bobby and his mother came up the walk, Grandfather continued in his usual fashion, running on about ice houses and polar bears and walruses, throwing his arms about in all directions and striking one silly pose after another, but suddenly I did not mind: he was talking. The silence was gone.

He convinced Bobby's mother to stop for a cup of coffee, leaving Bobby and me alone on the verandah. Bobby had perfected the art of not imposing. He squatted down and stared contentedly at the two beetles I had been watching earlier. I was relieved not to have to make small talk, and after watching him stare at the beetles with such complete absorption for a moment or two, I found myself kneeling down to join him. A moment or two after that I found myself explaining how they moved in relation to the sun.

For the first time I saw how any discovery, large or small, affected him. It broke over him like a wave on a beach. He rocked back on his heels, his mouth and eyes wide open, but it was not just a matter of his exaggerated physical response. More striking was the feeling that he had been washed clean and his whole world re-organized. He crouched there, transfixed, his mouth seemingly stuck open, and for a moment I was ready to accept the town's verdict about him. It was easy to think of him as The Wriggler or That Poor Unfortunate Scott Boy. It even crossed my mind that I had caused some sort of fit and that he was going to begin to slobber or something worse. But before I could become a firm believer in the town's judgment of him, and perhaps never see him any other way again, he spoke.

"They use the sun the way sailboats use the wind."

He looked up at me and smiled as if he had just accomplished something momentous. I started to make the kind of bland non-committal remark you make to a drunk or a religious pamphleteer in order to get by him and on with your business, but I stopped in mid-sentence. Suddenly what he had said—not how it had been said, or who I thought was saying it, but what he had actually said—came home to me. It was my turn to rock back on my heels with amazement. The metaphor was slightly askew, but it was also very right, and by not expecting even an average reply I had almost missed a perceptive one. I looked at him closely. It was like discovering a secret that everyone else had missed.

I think I now understand more clearly why his statement amazed me. Regardless of what people said about him or how ridiculous he looked as he squatted there, Bobby had taken what I had said, reasoned with it and then given it back to me greater than it was before. It was a rare experience for me. I sat still, probably for as long as he had sat, trying to think of a reply that would keep the conversation going. I probably looked as foolish as he had looked. Then I held up my hand, casting a shadow on the two beetles, and they both stopped in confusion. I spoke, "And if you block out the wind, they can't sail." Bobby smiled as brightly as before, and I smiled right back at him with the same lunatic intensity.

It was at that precise moment when the seeds of our friendship were planted. Together we had built something out of words, each making a contribution. I am tempted to say that it was the first real conversation I had ever had with someone of my own age. I suppose there must have been others who went beyond saying, "Jeez, Corning, where do you find that weird stuff," or "Sure Corning, whatever you say," but I have also stood in enough theatre lobbies, cocktail parties and committee meetings to know that a real conversation is truly rare.

I looked up. The street seemed less raw than it had when I first came outside. Its edges were less sharp. I leaned back against the wall of the house. Bobby did the same. I clasped my arms around my knees. Bobby echoed my movement and we sat there smiling. The sun was warm; the world, or at least Union, suddenly seemed possible.

When my grandparents and Jennifer-Rose came back out on the verandah, Bobby and I were still talking. Of course I was doing most of the talking, as was always to be the case, but Bobby was truly there and not floating around in some world of his own as most of the townspeople would have assumed. My grandfather noticed right away that the geometry had changed.

"There you are, young lady. I told you they would get along. We are going to be fine."

"Are you sure it's no trouble for you?" She was looking at my grandfather but I could tell she was speaking to my grandmother. It was Grandmother who answered.

"I have been married to Roderick long enough, Mrs. Scott, to know that if there should be trouble, it will probably not be the fault of either of the boys."

"Well I suppose it would be all right then. It would be fine if he would stay around the Hotel, but he always wanders off with the other boys. I can't really blame him." Grandfather took it all as settled.

"Good enough Jennifer. The deal is closed. You better get along. If you are going to draw a wage, then you better put in the hours is what I always say."

She turned to Bobby. "Bobby, you are going to spend the rest of the day with Jonathan and Mr. Caldwell. If I hear of any problem there will be more than words when I get home. Do you understand?" Bobby nodded vigorously. She grabbed him on one of his upward swings and kissed him on the top of his head.

Grandmother went back inside, and Jennifer-Rose started off to work. Grandfather, Bobby and I watched her go. She had a nice way of walking. It was somehow both relaxed and efficient, the result, I suppose, of her job as a waitress and barmaid. It was not a sway or a wiggle or any of the other descriptions often applied to a woman's walk. She walked as if she did not care if the whole town was watching, and she also walked as if she did not care if anyone at all was watching. Indeed, the way she walked was probably as good an example as anything else of the quality in her that bothered many of the townspeople of Union.

Her story was as easy to come by as anyone else's in Union, perhaps easier, and the gossip about her was increased even further that summer by Bobby and me. Eight years before, Robert Scott, her husband, and one of the more popular young men in the town, had deserted her. He "flew south and didn't come back" is how my grandfather phrased it. Regardless of the fact that it had been Jennifer who had been wronged, most of the town tended to side with her husband. The story ran that one of the main points of difference between them was Jennifer's stubborn resistance to sending Bobby to "the kind of place where he could receive proper care." Whether that truly was the problem or not was unimportant, however, because she had then compounded her error by seeking employment in Union and commencing to raise Bobby on her own rather than doing the right thing by going back to live in the seclusion of her parents' farm. At the very least, she could have moved to the comfortable anonymity of the city. I suspect the job she took also weighed against her, regardless of the fact that there was no other job available. Jim Houghton had given her a position that was a combination barmaid, chambermaid and part-time cook at the Union Hotel. It was a hard job, and she had further complicated the whole matter by doing it well.

My strongest sense of her was that she was accessible. Of course, I do not mean she was accessible in the same way as it was meant in the rumours. I suppose what I do mean is that you could talk to her. She spoke, but she listened as well. She did not have the same patina that most other adults had developed. Still, her biggest sin was evident that day right there in the way she walked. It was plain that she owed nothing to anyone. My grandfather said it in his own way as she crossed the street.

"Gentlemen, you tell a lot about people and horses by the way they walk. There is a lot of dance in that one, but she goes straight ahead and doesn't shy a bit."

She paused on the far side of the street and turned and waved to us. It was not a princess-from-a-car kind of wave. It was more like a salute. Grandfather called out to her. "Well young lady, next time you see us we should have it all tied down and ready to travel."

Anyone else would have asked what was to be tied down, but she just smiled and called back to us. "I don't doubt you will, Mr. Caldwell, but I wonder if the town is ready for it." Now I sometimes wonder if, with her experience of the town, she caught a glimpse of what might be in store for us.

We watched her out of sight, and then Grandfather sat down in his chair and spoke. "The day lies before us gentlemen. Any suggestions?"

We said nothing.

"Right you are, boys. Always weigh your words. My father used to say that a man who speaks off the cuff is gonna end up looking kind of frayed." He paused for a moment, looked out at the street and then continued. "It has occurred to me, Jonathan, that after your inauspicious introduction to Union, and your brush with the ice machine Bob, that we could lay over for a day to rest the horses and wash our socks. We could just sit up here and let the world come to us."

He looked over at us again. It was clearly our opportunity to vote for remaining at the house over whatever else he had in mind, but we remained silent. He leaned forward on his chair and then stood up.

"Well, I guess you are right. There has been too much laying back lately. It's time we went to work. Maybe we better go downtown and see how the old burg is holding together. I haven't been down for quite a while myself, and I was kind of skittish yesterday. What do you say Bob? Shall we show the city slicker here the sights?"

Bobby nodded and smiled.

"Parade the flag?"

Bobby nodded again, harder.

"Take us a little stroll down Main Street?"

"Yessir, Mr. Caldwell. Let's go downtown."

Grandfather turned and called into the house. "Ruby, me and the boys have come to a decision. If you would grace our presence, I have an announcement to make."

My grandmother came out on the verandah drying her hands on her apron. Every time Grandfather made one of his announcements, my grandmother dried her hands on her apron. I think it was her way of denying my grandfather the kind of shocked response he often tried to elicit. I admired her technique a good deal.

"Ruby, me and the boys here have come to a decision." He paused. "We have decided that Jonathan had better get the lay of the land if he is going to spend time in Union. We intend to give him the complete $5 tour." He waited, looking at her or perhaps looking for something from her. He cleared his throat. "It has occurred to me that when the sun reaches its zenith we might still be engaged. I figure we will have lunch at the nearest convenient spot."

He had hit the mark. "Rod, if that spot happens to be the café, I don't want these boys eating anything from that grill."

Grandfather reacted as if she had given a blessing to the venture. Suddenly he was moving us down the steps, talking as he went. "Never fear, Ruby, never fear. Their lips shall touch nothing that has touched that grill." When we reached the gate she called out. I had expected it. I knew she was going to give him some further caution about not keeping me out too late or encouraging me to use bad language or one of the other multitude of sins he might teach me. She did not mention me at all.

"Rod, don't you stop at the Hardware. You know what he said." She was looking down at us, plainly concerned and trying to cover it up with an irritable tone of voice.

"Everyone in the whole town knows what he said Ruby. But do not trouble yourself. I shall avoid the Hardware religiously." He gave it a two-beat pause. "For today anyways." He had begun to smile openly as if he had finally got the response he was looking for. "But it has occurred to me this morning, Ruby, that sooner or later, my responsibility as a chaperone for young Jonathan here might require me to pick up a few odds and ends. But not today. There is a time and place for everything. Right gentlemen?" I have to admit that there was something infectious in his smile. He looked at the two of us closely. "Well, I guess you will pass muster."

He swung the gate open. "The world awaits us, boys. Shall we set forth? All for one and one for all." Bobby smiled, and skeptical though I was whenever he began to put on a show, I straightened up a bit as we stepped out onto the street.

We set forth.

I am not quite sure about all the ingredients that go into "setting forth," but heroes, adventurers and other storybook characters set forth in almost every story I read. Bold adventure had to be in the offing, or perhaps a brave attempt at a feat lesser mortals would shrink from. My grandfather was the only person outside of a fairytale I ever saw manage it properly.

I suppose in our own way we were making a brave attempt that day. Bobby and I knew that we might run into Wayne or one of his friends and that the consequences might be unpleasant. It must have been an equally important journey for my grandfather; it was the first time he had been downtown in weeks if you did not count the aborted journey of the day before. I now wonder how much of his performance that day was simply bravado. In any case, it was a journey we were to make almost every day of that summer, and every time it seemed new. Often we set forth, but many times we set sail. Other times we sallied out. Sometimes we simply strolled down. But the one thing that every single one of those journeys had in common was that the towns-people, and certainly Bobby and me, were carried along by Grandfather's performance.

Even that summer I knew that my grandfather was often dismissed as a "character," and with the keen social consciousness of a twelve-year-old about such matters, I was usually dismayed by it. But not on those trips downtown. However he was labelled, there was something about him, something about his way of seeing things, which made each trip into a kind of parade. We would step out on the street and Mary Kent and her sister Jodie would stop whatever mysterious girl's pastime they were engaged in, and for a moment their supreme ten-year-old self-possession would be shaken as they wondered if what they were doing was really the most important and interesting activity in the world after all. The Morris' german shepherd, lying on his porch in the morning heat would not only raise his head to watch us, but he would even thump his tail once or twice in acknowledgment of our passage. Mrs. Rose from across the street, out for a moment to pour the remainder of her mid-morning tea on her flowerbed, would place her hand on the brim of her sun-bonnet and smile as we passed by.

Grandfather was a born parade marshall. I am convinced that given the slightest excuse he would have happily carried one of those big batons, and twirling it, stepped out in front of us. He was the retired actor returned to the stage to play his last great role. He gestured histrionically, stopped dead to stare intently, paused to digress largely, posed to point dramatically and each of his gestures was just slightly larger than was required for Bobby and me. He was playing to the town.

The role that brought him out of retirement was, I suppose, the only one that could have supported such excess: the wise, humourous, slightly eccentric grandfather imparting his wisdom to the apple-cheeked boys of summer. He did it superbly. Even that first day I think everyone who saw us recognized the role, at least unconsciously, and smiled approvingly upon it: "Good to see you up and about again Rod," or "Guess I am gonna have to keep my wife at home again, ha ha," or "As long as you're out and about Rod, see if you can get us some rain." Many people just smiled benignly at us as if we were some sort of animated Norman Rockwell print. Grandfather accepted any and all tributes graciously: "I got to show these boys what kind of show we run around here," he would call back.

Bobby and I understood what was happening. Children have a fine sense of role-playing and performance. We certainly did not mind. It was a plain and simple joy for Grandfather to be back on the street, and he communicated that joy.

In fact, as the summer progressed, I came to recognize that every single person in town made an equivalent journey at some point in the day or the week. At any time of the day you could see someone going down to Main Street, and undoubtedly if you stopped one of them, they would have had an excuse ready. Mrs. Bosker, a contemporary of my grandmother's who lived two houses up the street, could be seen every morning at 9.30 making a casual progress down the street, stopping and talking to people on the sidewalk or on their verandahs, holding her net shopping-bag over her arm as if it were her admission ticket to the show. Later in the morning, if you called out to Mr. Timson he would always smile and wave, holding up one or two envelopes so you would understand he was on his way to the post office to carry on a correspondence he had been having with other stamp collectors for over fifteen years. In the heat of the mid-afternoon, small children would brandish empty pop bottles back at their mothers and call out they were going to Elliot's General Store. Later in the afternoon a teenaged boy or girl would cite the café and a milkshake as a destination. Union was like a giant clock face with innumerable hands sweeping around it at set intervals, and regardless of what each person's excuse was, their real reason for heading toward Main Street was to see and be seen, talk and be talked to. My grandfather said it with enormous satisfaction that day as we set forth.

"Romans had their baths, boys. We have Main Street. It's business, pure and simple. It's the business of the world."

The first stop we made that day was no more than a block and a half down from my grandparents' house. It was a large weathered building that had two garage-type doors at the front. One of them was closed and one of them was open. Grandfather had folded his arms and was staring into the shadowed interior. He had his hand to his chin, and if he had had a beard he would have been stroking it. Bobby was staring inside as well. He was smiling. Grandfather spoke.

"Well, Bobby, what do you think? Should we show him the Collection?"

Bobby nodded.

"Yes. I suppose you are right. No tour of Union can start without a look at the Collection." He peered into the building and raised his voice as he continued. "I figure we better warn him about Barstow. He is a bit off at times, Jonathan. I'll say it straight out. Jerome Barstow has one or two queer notions. For example, just what do you figure we are looking at right now. What kind of establishment would you say this is?"

According to the three signs on the front I had three choices. BLACKSMITH had been painted front and centre in letters a foot high, well above the garage doors. I could see that the paint that had been used had once been of a dark colour, but it had faded. The remnants of the letters did not provide a visual impression so much as the tactile sense that the letter-shaped spaces where the paint had once been were slightly less eroded by wind and sun.

Immediately below BLACKSMITH, just at the height that someone might reach while standing on a stepladder, the word WELDER had been painted on. The lettering was still professional looking, but it was slightly smaller. It had obviously been painted on at a much later date, but it too had begun to fade, and in a few years would disappear over the same horizon as BLACKSMITH. Finally, painted on the garage door that was closed was the sign, "Tall Repairs, Small Repairs, All Repairs." It did not look more than a few years old, and each of the letters was surrounded by a faint spray of green paint suggesting it had been stencilled more carelessly than the other two signs. I wondered if the collection they had referred to meant the signs. I decided upon the middle sign. "I guess it's a welding shop."

"Good for you. Always take the middle road is what I say. Of course, sooner or later Barstow is going to tell you different. It's one of his queer notions. Get him in the right mood and he is going to tell you that what you are looking at right now is nothing less than the birthplace of civilization. Now I have a slight disagreement about that, but it makes a pretty good story. It goes like this..."

Before he could begin, however, one last sign walked out of the green shadows of the building. "Used Goods for Sale. Used means USEFUL." had been painted free-hand on a piece of plyboard, and it was being carried by a man. He leaned the sign up against the open door and then turned to us. I cannot be completely sure at this distance in time, but I think Jerome Barstow was one of those people whom, from time to time in my life, I have liked upon first sight. The first thing I noticed was the brown stetson and one of those pencil-thin moustaches. With no preamble whatsoever he began to upbraid my grandfather.

"Rod, you have got more nerve than even I gave you credit for. Not only are you getting set to steal my story, but you are doing it right on my own doorstep."

Neither my grandfather nor Bobby seemed taken aback by him. Bobby continued to smile and my grandfather spoke. "Jonathan, it looks like you get the chance to meet Union's one and only blacksmith. Jerome, meet my grandson."

He came up to me and shook my hand. "How are you Jonathan. I heard you were in town." He pushed his hat back on his head. "Bobby, you brought me some business this morning. I guess both you boys did. Jim Houghton came in, and he wants a bar across the mouth of that ice machine of his. What in the world were you doing back there? I have told you a dozen times if you want to do some exploring, you stop by and do it here."

"Yes, Mr. Barstow." Bobby looked properly abashed, and Mr. Barstow stared at him a moment before he shifted his stetson again and continued speaking.

"Well there is no use in standing out here and getting addled by the sun. There are some among us who can't afford to get anymore addled than they already are. Come on in."

"Well, seeing as how you are your usual gracious self, Blacksmith, I guess we might as well. Come on, boys, at least you can pick up on that commission, unless he was just talking through his stetson."

Bobby and I stood in the shadows just inside the door and listened to the exchange that continued between the two of them. It was blustery and argumentative, but I realized they were friends. I was slightly disconcerted to hear someone keep pace with my grandfather.

"It's been a while, Rod. I figured you had just about given up on everything south of your fence line. I was actually figuring I would brave Ruby's crusade to straighten me out and come up and visit you."

"I have been lying fallow, Jerome, just lying fallow. Even good soil needs a rest now and then."

119

"I will let that pass. What brings you out now besides the fact that you haven't stolen one of my stories for a while."

"Well, Jerome, I decided it was the responsibility of those of my generation to give the younger generation here the benefit of our experience. I figured I better make sure they know how to keep the show rolling."

"You figure that you know something that they need to know. I am not so sure." There was a pause, and I thought for a moment he was using Grandfather's technique. Instead, he appeared to change the subject. "I heard from Henry."

"A letter?"

"Yep."

"Where from?"

"Take a look for yourself. I already put it on the pop cooler. Hey Bobby."

"Yes Mr. Barstow."

"I guess while it's open you and Jonathan might as well have a bottle. We'll call it your commission. Just leave that back row alone."

Bobby and I walked halfway down the side of the shop and he positioned me in front of the pop cooler. He was smiling and beginning to wave about slightly. It was clear to me that I was supposed to be surprised by something. He opened the lid. I was surprised.

The lid of the pop cooler was literally papered over with beer labels. They were assembled there like a page of graduation photographs in a yearbook. Bobby was smiling and bobbing up and down, and my grandfather was watching me closely for my reaction as well. If they were anticipating speechlessness, that is certainly what they got. I stepped up and looked closer. There must have been almost a hundred of them, and no two were alike. Some were printed in English and some were not. Some were all lettering and others were just pictures. There were portraits of men in plumed hats and Indians in head-dresses and soldiers in golden helmets and knights in armour. There were a variety of lions and cougars and panthers, and there was a scattering of birds and deer and bears. There were a few creatures that were either mythological or simply poorly rendered. There were mountain scenes and lake scenes and forest scenes and sea shores. The labels had been varnished over to protect them, and it gave them a translucence. Later that summer I learned that, stared at long enough, they almost became windows. Other times they could become maps. That day I simply stared, hypnotized by the contradiction between the chaos of colours and pictures and the orderly, label by label progress of them all. Regardless of how garish each individual label was, taken together they achieved a sovereignty, like the rows of brilliantly embroidered merit badges on the tunics of the two eagle scouts who always visited the school on Remembrance Day to carry the flag.

Mr. Barstow had come up behind me. He spoke. "You just met my son Henry, Jonathan. He sends me new ones back every time he gets the chance."

I looked back and up. Mr. Barstow was staring at the labels. It was as if he did not want to be intrigued but could not help it.

"That is about all I ever see of him, too. Down there on the bottom right, Rod, the last one in the row."

Grandfather leaned down and stared at the label. It was a cactus painted in bright green. It sat in a pinkish desert.

"Mexico?"

"Yep."

"I thought he said Texas."

"I guess it's a Texas operation, but they were drilling somewhere across the border in Mexico. He didn't write much. Just a note with the label saying he would write when he had time."

"Well, I guess he will have a few stories when he gets back. When do you think that'll be?"

"You know Henry, Rod. He will come when he comes.

He will have a few more stories and a few more labels and not much else."

"Could be worse."

"Sure it could. He could forget the labels."

"The boy is seeing the world Jerome. You want him to come back here and spend his time sitting in this shop? It might be fine for us, but he is a young man."

Mr. Barstow re-settled his stetson and shrugged, "Whatever. Anyways, I'd better let Jonathan here know what he is up against." He turned to me. "Your grandfather is an old bandit, Jonathan. Take it from me. I have known him longer than you have, and I have to tell you that he is the worst outlaw I have ever encountered." The description seemed so apt to me that I started to smile. Mr. Barstow stopped speaking, and he looked at me closely. I probably should have been intimidated, but I was not. He slowly started to smile in return.

"Your grandfather was about to fill your head with some nonsense about the first blacksmith I made the mistake of telling him years ago. The old Greeks called him Hephaestus. Fact of the matter is that my own mother had to fight tooth and nail to keep my father from branding me with it. This Hephaestus was a Greek god and they credited him with starting civilization. He was a master of earthly fire. My father used to tell me the whole story. Your grandfather has taken to re-writing it to suit himself, and sooner or later he is going to run it by you that a merchant is the one who started the ball rolling and not a blacksmith. Of course, he is dead wrong. The Greeks didn't have a merchant god as far as I know. But if you start listening to him he will have you believing they had some god named Woolworth up there on Mount Olympus. But if you want the real story, you just come to me."

It was clear to me that they had had the argument of Blacksmith versus Merchant many times before. It was also clear that in stopping when he did he was giving my grandfather a free opening, something that Grandfather would have had to work hard for with my grandmother. Grandfather settled back in his chair and pulled out a cigar. I had seen the same look on his face many times before. He was enjoying himself.

"I guess that would have made you Festus for short. Interesting name. Festus. Not too common. Hephaestus Barstow. Kind of has a ring to it. Matter of fact you might say it clangs like a fire engine. It is curious. You know a man for years and then one day you find..."

"Just run it out as far as you like. It is not going to change anything. The story still stands. It was a blacksmith and not a merchant."

"Hold on a second Blacksmith. Just let me speak my piece. I have seen the whole thing with my own eyes. In other words I have it on personal authority. I saw this town before it was even a bend in the road and it didn't grow up around any unpainted welder's shop."

"You are right there. It was the railroad. I don't recall it, but I suppose you are going to claim that C, P and R stand for Customer, Price and Receipt."

"No I am not going to claim it was the railroad. I have heard enough about that gawddamned railroad. People talk like some line of track woke up one morning and said to itself 'I think I will grow out to Union,' then some engine said to itself, 'I think I will puff on up there with you and build a station.' No sir. I tell you what it was..."

"Yep. I know. You figure it was a bunch of merchants. Well let me tell you I am a bit confused. You are going to tell me that it was merchants who financed the railroad, which in turn started the town. But just how many times have I heard you curse the railroad. Now, just how do you put those two things together."

Grandfather looked at his cigar. He had not yet lit it. "Trade routes, Jerome, trade routes. Railroad is just a tool we happen to have right now. It doesn't matter if it is camels or pack horses or ships. We can talk about the silk route or the spice route or the discovery of the whole show back in 1492. It is all based on some merchant selling his goods and spreading the story of the world. Any farm wife will tell you that the old pedlars who used to come by were dealing in more than pots and thread. They spread the news, Blacksmith. Trade routes and the news of the world. Trade routes, Blacksmith. Trade routes are the roots of civilization. And by gawd I should write that down."

"I missed you. The last couple of weeks I even considered getting myself a televison, but now that you are back on the line I guess I won't have to. Whatever else you are, you are sure as hell entertaining when you get wound up."

"You know, every time I detect that note of insincerity in your voice I figure I have you up against it. Well, you better think fast, Blacksmith, because sarcasm lasts only so long against logic. I am holding the trade routes and the news of the world in my hand. Just what do you figure you can put on the table to beat it?"

"I think I know you at least as well as you know me. And when I hear that after-dinner-cigar tone in your voice I know I am halfway there because not once have you ever picked the right place to sit back. There are a couple of things you better clarify for me. You have been hotfooting it around the world from China to Spain. You have been travelling through a range of at least a thousand years. Why don't we just slow it down here for a second or two. You have got railroads and camels and ships, but if we just pull over to the side of the trade route here for a second and unpack one of those camels, take a look in the hold and what have you got? Just what was it they were trading? Unless I miss my guess, Merchant, we are going to unpack something some fellow made on a forge."

The exchange continued. At any other place and time I would have been happy just to sit and listen to it. It was not just that I had encountered someone who could keep up with my grandfather, although that was a revelation to me. It was, besides, a simple pleasure to listen to. It was almost like a play. The nuances of their argument about the birth of civilization had obviously been polished over the years, but it was not a static exchange. There was a push and tug to it, they sat forward and back in their chairs. The excitement was not counterfeit. But Bobby was tugging at my sleeve and asking me if I wanted to see the collection. I was puzzled.

"Didn't I just see it?"

"There is more, Jonathan, if you want to look at it."

It is difficult to describe the effect that Barstow's shop had on me that day as I followed Bobby around it. From the inside it was more the size and shape of a barn than it appeared to be from the outside. If it had been empty, I suppose there would have been space for two cars parked end to end on either half of it. As it was, the right half's door was always closed and that half of the building and the two sheds that adjoined it were filled, at times to the rafters, with the things that Mr. Barstow had taken in trade or picked up at auctions, estate sales or building demolitions. On the long back wall of the shop there was a workbench and all of his tools, and at the centre of the back wall a large brick fireplace that I assume had served at some point as his forge.

Bobby and I started our exploration of the far side of the shop and the sheds at the back of the shop. There was a pathway cleared that ran around the huge, rafter-high pile of junk that was stacked in the centre of the right-hand side of the garage. Branches of this pathway also led into the corners and into the two sheds that were also piled high with everything from leaning coils of treadless tires to stacks of used magazines.

But general dimensions, even an inventory had it been possible, had little to do with the impression the place made. There was a backstage excitement about it. The open rafters were piled with odds and ends of lumber, plywood, drainpipes and sheet metal, but sitting up there, jumbled high in the shadows of the roof, they became more mysterious than they would have otherwise been. Similarly, the two washing-machines and three refrigerators, standing together in the dimness of the far front corner with parts of their insides spilling out on the floor, for the first time escaped their bland everyday whiteness and achieved the mystery and possibility of machines.

In contrast, sunlight, blued by the grimy windows, would randomly light upon articles and invest them with brilliant definition. The rusty leg-traps hanging on the back wall were picked out by the light so that just looking at them, the sharpness and the rust and the coiled steel strength were tangible. Such illumination was not just physical; it seemed to suggest that each item touched this way must have had a special and important history. Many of them did. That day the sun chose a wickerwork perambulator. It had been painted a glossy pink that was peeling on the handles to reveal a glossy blue beneath. Someone named Harold Boswood had been convinced of a boy, but his wife had presented him with a girl. In Mr. Barstow's shop it sat next to the far wall, and when touched by the sun it shone pink and amber, filled to the brim with empty beer bottles.

Beside the perambulator was a wooden box, each of its sides and its lid embellished by the same scene, pine trees, blue sky and a circling bird. From the back of the box a cord protruded. Inside, the box was vacant but for an empty light socket. After failing at three guesses, I was given the answer by Bobby. He told me it was a hawk-egg incubator put together by George Maclenan for his daughter. She had painted it and tried to hatch two red-tailed hawk's eggs in it when she was nine years old.

I began to wonder if everything in Barstow's had its own story, and as the bright hard-edged certainties alternated with the dim, shadowed possibilities, it began to seem as if we could not take a step without reaching to pick up some artifact of the town, talk about it, wonder about its purpose and history, and then carefully put it back. By the time we came all the way around the pathway and found ourselves standing by the door we had entered, I was completely disoriented. I was also disconcerted, because looking at the street reminded me of the actual size of the shop and the fact that we could not have travelled more than a hundred feet in total, and it had seemed ten times that far. Looking at the street reminded me of other things as well. After I found my bearings I spoke.

"I guess Wayne and the others hang around here a lot?"

Bobby shook his head.

"They don't? Jeez, why not? It's a lot better than the curling-rink."

"I'm the only one. Mr. Barstow won't let the others in his shop. I think he lets me in because he knew my father. He used to help Mr. Barstow and his son fix up cars." His reply had been addressed to the frayed end of an extension cord he was holding in his hands. I realized that something was bothering him and assumed it was the mention of his father. I thought it might be best to change the subject entirely, but I was very much taken with the fact that Wayne and Company were denied access to Barstow's. It made the place even more attractive to me.

I pretended to examine the street. Bobby was holding the extension cord at the plug end as if preparing to defend himself against any hostile sockets that might appear. He looked ridiculous, and once again I caught a glimpse of why so many people had dismissed him as less than normal. He looked up and caught me glancing at him. Perhaps there was something in my expression that prompted him to say what he then said.

"They are probably all over at the curling-rink, Jonathan. You can go if you want to. It's all right. They won't say anything to you. But they might if I go too, so I better not. Not today anyways. But you can go." He looked down at the plug in his hand and it was as if he saw it for the first time. "I have to put this back. Mr. Barstow doesn't like anything moved."

It took a few seconds for me to realize that he actually thought I wanted to go and see Wayne and the others. I could hardly believe it. At the same moment, however, I realized he had just made a far more generous offer than I could have made in similar circumstances.

I started after him. "Bobby, you don't think I want to go and hang around there with Wayne, do you?" As I said it I felt some surprise that I actually did not want to go there. "This place is better than a thousand curling-rinks."

He stopped, turned and looked at me. "Wayne says it's just a bunch of junk and he wouldn't come here if he could."

"Wayne is just jealous because he is not allowed in here. This place is..." I paused, at a loss to explain just what was so special about Mr. Barstow's shop. Then it came to me. "This place is just about the best I have ever seen for a club-house." I could see he did not understand. I sat down on an old wooden pop crate and tried to explain the finer points of clubhouses. But as I explained the joys of clubhousing and why Barstow's was a perfect location, I could tell I was not making myself understood. Whenever I paused and queried him with the time-honoured, "You know what I mean?" he could only reply with a less confident, "I guess so, Jonathan. Sure, I understand."

Perhaps it was my desire to make him truly understand that what we had was far better than Wayne's curling-rink that explains what happened next. I found myself telling him an unmodified version of my experience with the club-house in the bushes. It was not like the day before when I had thrown the mermaid to the other boys. My motives were different. I did not want to impress him as much as I simply wanted him to understand. Perhaps, too, there was something about Barstow's shop, or Bobby, which made it possible for me to try and tell him about the one perfect clubhouse in my experience.

When I finished telling Bobby, I realized for the first time what had been so special about the place I had seen. "Don't you see? It was complete. It was done right. Everybody does things halfway, but that place was done right. This place is kind of the same. Do you see? We could make a clubhouse here, and it would be all finished. It would be all complete. Do you know what I mean?"

Having told someone, I was almost desperate to be understood. Bobby had begun to nod and smile, and then he spoke. "I do Jonathan, I understand. I didn't. But now I do. I haven't shown you the best part. We don't even have to build one. It's already been done." He led me a few steps back into the piled up half of the shop, and pulled a tarp aside.

"It's right here."

It was my turn to be confused. I was looking at the back doors of some sort of panel van. I could see, in fact, that the central pile of articles in the shop was so high because it was stacked up on the vehicle, but I still did not understand what he was talking about. I was irritated, and still wondering if he was addled in some way.

"What is right there, Bobby? I don't understand what you are talking about."

He opened the door. "Our clubhouse."

I looked inside and then stepped up and part way in and looked more carefully. He was absolutely right. It may not have been the clubhouse in the bushes, but the 1948 Cadillac hearse that sat under the mouldering pile of odds and ends in Mr. Barstow's welding shop was, unmistakably, a complete and nearly perfect clubhouse.

I did not see all of its finer points that day, but we did use it as a kind of clubhouse that summer, and I came to know it very well. In the back it was all deep purple velvet. For the coffins, there were oak casters that whirled at the slightest touch for what seemed to be ages. There were two velvet-covered seats that folded up just behind the front seat, or could be left down and completely invisible unless you knew the right place to reach for them. It had served as an ambulance as well, and cots folded down from either wall. Between the fold-up chairs there was a small box fastened to the floor that could serve as a table and also opened for storage. The front seats had been removed. Mr. Barstow was in the process of re-upholstering them. The hearse had been the last project of Henry, his son, before he had started welding on oil rigs around the world, and Mr. Barstow liked to have it a little better each time Henry returned. There was a side door as well as the door at the back, and it became our habit to roll that door back and listen to my grandfather and Mr. Barstow talk. We would look out past the tarpaulin that hung down over the opening and out past the piles of cardboard boxes and hanging garden hoses and legs of chairs stacked upside down, and it would be like looking out at the world from a cave in a wild but strangely civilized forest.

That first day, when Bobby opened the side door, we heard the final fragment of the conversation that had been going on since we had arrived. "Well, Blacksmith, I can see this will have to remain an open conversation. But I have got one more story before we go. I stole this one too, from a fellow named Prescott. Mr. Prescott wrote a book called *The Conquest of Peru...*"

"Prescott probably pinched it himself."

"That's right, Jerome. It's called History. Anyways, what do you figure the conquistadors shod their horses with when they ran out of iron?"

"You are going to tell me gold, Rod, but I don't buy it. You are talking to someone who knows metal and gold is too soft. You are slipping. You have been lying around too long."

"As a matter of fact, Blacksmith, I was not going to say gold. They didn't use gold for precisely the reason you have just cited. They used silver. Now, what does that story tell you?"

"Tells me I would rather have one of the horseshoes."

"Well, what it says to me Jerome is that you take it where you find it."

"I have been doing that half my life, Rod."

"Come on boys, time we got back on track."

We paused at the door after all the goodbyes had been said.

"One other thing it tells me, Jerome. You have to use what comes to hand."

"Okay Rod. My only question is whether it's true or not. The story is not much good if you just cooked it up."

My grandfather looked back into the shop. "Of course it's true Jerome. A good storyteller always tells the truth." He gave it a three-beat pause. "That way, when he has to lie, people will believe him."

Main Street and Beyond

As we moved down the street, closer and closer to the point where I had seen the town unravel on the day before, it filled me with the Funhouse suspense you feel when you know the skeleton will dangle down, but you are not sure when. The fence that had started it all was across the street and down no more than half a block. We moved toward it slowly. It seemed we were stopping every ten or fifteen feet to exchange pleasantries with one of the townspeople or to hear one of Grandfather's Guided Tour routines about the first streetlight in Union, his role in establishing the town library or the advantages of boardwalks over sidewalks. Although I continued to appear interested in what he was discoursing upon and made the appropriate gestures when introduced to the people who stopped us, I was really concerned with our gradual approach to the fence.

Finally we were immediately opposite to it, talking to yet another of my grandfather's acquaintances, but still it stubbornly refused to alter. So, human nature being what it is, I stubbornly began to try and make it change. I tried glancing at it out of the corner of my eye in the hopes it could be tricked into revealing itself. It refused. Like someone who is afraid of heights titillating himself by peering over ledges, I even squinted up my eyes and glanced at it, a technique I employed to change streetlights into star shapes, but the fence remained obstinately mundane. That it did not change was almost more unsettling than if it had. I felt let down, I cannot say why, and in the ensuing emotional lull, I began to notice that my grandfather was worrying.

He slowed down and then came to a full stop in front of the War Memorial. He started, then he stopped again. Then he turned and walked into the memorial.

"I figure we better re-group right here gentlemen, close ranks now or they will pick us off one by one when we hit Main Street." He sat down on the steps of the cairn. "And if I have to smile at one more person I will probably just give up, start kissing babies and become a politician." He pulled out his cigars and began preparations to light one. I decided that Bobby was a sufficient audience for the ritual, and I began to examine the Memorial. There was not much to see. The caragana hedge ticked in the heat, and the grass was thick, long and untrodden. The whole enclosure, perhaps 50 feet across, had an official and unused air about it that made me reluctant to walk on the grass. There were gaps in the hedge so that the Memorial would always be visible no matter how untrimmed the hedge became, but the sense of enclosure was maintained by arcs of thin chain going from post to post around the entire memorial. For want of something better to do I began reading the plaques on the cairn.

On the front was the plaque for the First War. There were

six names of those who served from Sortie River County. On the next side over there were the names for World War Two, but I noticed a plaque on the back with a more interesting inscription, and I moved around to read it. I had no sooner begun than I heard my grandfather on the other side of the cairn exhale and speak. "Read that one out loud for us, Jonathan."

I stifled a desire to ask him how he knew what I was looking at and began to read. "In memory of Jessie Loudon Coyne and Ronald Davis Crewes, young flyers who were stayed by the hand of death while on a training mission over the Sortie River valley on 15 July, 1941. We shall remember their flight." I came back around the cairn. Grandfather, perhaps influenced by the stillness of the War Memorial enclosure, attempted a smoke ring that failed. He began to speak.

"Guess I have seen a fair number of War Memorials in my time. You have to figure that if a place the size of Union has got one then there must be a fair number dotted around. I have seen them for the local boys who died, seen them for death at sea, death in the air, death on the ground. I have seen them for the unknown soldier, the unknown sailor, the unknown airman. The fact of the matter is that they are all pretty much the same. They all have this kind of waiting-room feel about them no matter how big the trees are or how green the grass or whether the stone is marble or granite. But I will tell you something boys. Right here where we are sitting is the only place in the country, probably the whole damned world, where you are going to find a memorial for those who died while landing on a herd of Black Angus cattle." He was pretending to look off into the distance, but he ruined the effect by taking a quick glance down at us to see if he had us. He did.

"The airplane had been coming over every evening about the same time for close to two weeks. We had been told they were gonna be up there. They said they were teaching aerial reconnaissance and things like that. It was kind of the evening's entertainment. We would hear that drone and we'd all look up. Frank Elliot always said, 'Look up and smile folks, they're taking our picture.' It was funny for the first two times he said it, anyways. At first the kids waved at it like it was a train. Some of the adults, too. Of course nobody ever waved back. After the first week we were all pretty casual about air traffic. Some folks had even started saying how it ruined the evening sky for them. I figured the other way. I liked it. It kind of deepened the sky for me. Made it less flat. I think most felt all right about it. Anyways, we were all pretty cosmopolitan about airplanes by the time it happened." He checked the ash on his cigar, probably contemplated a brief digression on the Air Age, and then decided to continue.

"I guess I have heard my share of engines stall in my time. I have heard tractors quit with 50 acres left to plough. I have heard combines quit when a man has to get his crop in. I even had a '32 Dodge pickup quit everytime Ruby climbed in and that is a fact. But by gawd, I never heard anything like when that airplane quit running. Strangest damned things went through my head. Sounds like a little engine trouble I said to myself. Take care of your equipment and it'll take care of you. All the jackass things you say when some machine stops on you. And then suddenly I was realizing that I wasn't hearing some fella climb out lift the hood and start to cuss. And suddenly I am realizing that I am holding my breath and that I can't hear one sound in the whole damned town and I am watching that plane float through that blue sky and down over the bluff into the river valley. It must have been the quietest 60 seconds I ever heard in this town. I saw Elizabeth Wells and Frank Boychuck out on the street kind of stop in mid-sentence like they were posing for a photograph. Damn. It was the strangest thing. Bobby, have you ever broken something that was special to your mother?"

"Yessir."

"I mean something really special. Knocked it off the mantelpiece or the dining-room table."

"I broke her pocket watch, I mean my father's. I used to open it up and listen to it."

"Right. That's good. Now think about it. The exact moment when it dropped."

Bobby looked off for a moment. He sucked in his breath and his eyes grew wide.

"That's right, mister. You got it. Now figure a whole town like that. People stopped mid-sentence, cups halfway to mouths, hoes raised over garden weeds, mid-stride on Main Street, papers half picked up, cards half snapped down. Even the dogs quiet at all the sucked in breath. Listen... Listen for it... WHUMP. Not a bang, more like something ripping. I started for the Ford, but some folks just jumped. Didn't think. Didn't say anything. Just started to move. Jerome Barstow came firing out of his shop like it was the hundred-yard dash. That is the kind of sound it was. Don't think. Move. Barstow is one of the most level-headed men in this town and he went by the house like he was gonna run the whole way to the river. I caught up with him just the other side of the tracks. We were the first out. We swung down over the rise and saw it." He paused and carefully relit his cigar. Then he continued.

"They tried to come down on Rose's pasture. Back then Alistair was still alive and they were still farming. Was a good choice in some ways. Best piece of river bottom for 50 miles. Flat as a paved road and never touched by a plough. Anna Rose used to graze her cattle on it. Fence posts sprouted branches on that piece of dirt, but Anna would never let Alistair touch it. I guess he figured it was a small price to keep her happy. She used to raise those cattle like housepets. Gave them all names. Well it was something to see. It was that evening light, kind of thick and gold. Black smoke pumping up like a thunderhead. Cattle all pushed up at one end and we could see Anna just standing there and watching it burn.

"Funny thing, driving down that river hill. It was like...I don't know. It was like going to the circus. No. It was like when I was a boy and the big surf would come in on the north wind and it would be blowing so that you had to shout to hear and every time one of those big waves peeled over the point you had to jump and shout. I damn near started to whoop. No better than Barstow coming out of his shop like a rocket. It didn't make sense, but there it is. I was so damn hopped up I almost didn't make it around the curve before the bridge.

"But that left as soon as we got out to Anna. She was dog sick and white as a sheet. She was barely talking sense. She kept repeating herself. 'I molly coddled them, Rod. I brought them up like children. Sell them off tomorrow.' She kept repeating it. 'I will sell them off tomorrow, I swear I will.' Seems like they got that airplane well and down and the cattle were panicked and peeling off to either side when one of them cut back. She said it was like they just nicked him, but the plane went right over and exploded. Anna Rose was a regular church-going woman and she just stood there and swore. Gawddamned airplane, gawddamned stupid beasts, gawddamned war. I couldn't figure out if she was mad at the cattle or the airplane or both. Barstow went and got an old horse blanket I kept in the trunk to wrap the jack in and he put it around her and she just sat down, pulled that dirty old thing over her head and bawled.

"There wasn't anything to do but wait for the fire to go out and then look to the bodies. We didn't even have to kill the steer. It'd been sliced up like it was through a meat grinder. Half the town was down on the pasture by then. The other half was up on the bluff. So we had our War. For five minutes it came over and landed right in Union. It wasn't pretty. It didn't smell good. It smelled like a rendering factory smells. It smelled like fuel oil and burnt hair.

Yep, war landed on Union on 15 July, 1941 and it smelled bad enough to make you lose your supper." He paused and shifted his back against the cairn. This time his gaze into the distance was legitimate. After a while he spoke once more, and his voice was more for himself than for us.

"Now here comes the good part boys. When the cameras stop clicking is when the real story always begins. There was a lot of feeling in town about those two young fellas who died in the airplane. A lot of feeling. But there was something else going on too. Something a bit out of whack. Missing on one piston. It was right there that first evening and we could have seen it plain if we had any sense. Walt Foster came ripping down the road about fifteen minutes after everybody else, put the brakes on so that the car almost rolled over and came running up to where we were all standing. 'Men,' he says, 'men, I have just talked to the commander. We are not to touch anything until they can get down here to view the scene and assess the situation.' Assess the situation. Gawddamn. There was something in the way Foster said that. It was like the whole world had fallen into place for him. He started strutting around. Said we should 'mount a guard.'

"I guess most of us figured he was just letting off steam. We were all pretty jumped up. The thing is, Foster didn't come down. And a whole lot of others besides. For the next few days there was a lot of talk about rights and duties and sacred obligations and a lot of other high-sounding words. Yep, it was like a fair all right, everybody right up on their toes. Can't say I wasn't myself. When they all got together on this plaque business it was me who wrote the words. 'Stayed by the hand of death.' Jesus, those two boys were stayed by a Black Angus steer. Helen Stadler got all the kids at school to take up a collection. Foster spent his time on Main Street talking about citizen militia, constant vigilance and a lot of other horseshit that wouldn't even grow wild oats. There was even a plan for a torch-light parade to unveil the plaque. We were gonna do it up right, no question about it. Whole damn town lost their brains for two weeks. I remember asking Foster how it was that he could spend all his time downtown with a filling-station to run up at the other end of First Street. I remember he looked at me and said, 'Roderick Caldwell, my duty to my country comes first.' Sweet Jesus." He fumbled for a match, lit his cigar again and I believe I thought he was done with the story. He was not.

"What the hell. Jonathan, move around the side there and read out the names on the plaque for World War Two." I walked to the side and squinted up at the plaque. There was no inscription, just the designation 1939-1945 followed by three names: Stanley Bourne, Robert Reeve Carson, Steven Walter Foster.

"All three of those boys signed up within a week of the fuss. When it came time for it, we didn't have the nerve to put any fancy words down, just the names. Foster's boy didn't even make it to Europe. He got killed when a tank rolled over him down at Camp Borden in Ontario."

The caragana hedge ticked and rustled in the heat. The colour seemed washed out of the day. I thought about the story I had told to Bobby back at Barstow's. I wondered if Grandfather had ever told anyone the story of the airplane before. For a moment the people standing on the bluff looking down at the crash and the neighbourhood children looking down at the bushes earlier in the spring seemed superimposed. Although 1941 seemed in the dim past to me, I suddenly wondered about the people Grandfather had mentioned and who they were and where they were. I looked over at Bobby. His knees were up to his chin and he was staring straight out to the street. The thought crossed my mind that if I stood up and walked to the entranceway, I could look across at the fence and it might begin to dissolve as it had the day before. I stayed where I was. Grandfather began to speak again.

"Funny thing about this damned memorial is that it really works. Nobody in this town ever comes near it. Probably for the same reason as me. You start to remember. Not that staying away helps much. It doesn't work like that. You can't fence a story out. A story has no great respect for a caragana hedge. That is what Barstow won't accept. There is a story in everything, and that's the thing that lasts. He tries to hedge himself in with that damned shop and I figure he comes pretty close to saying what he lets in and what he keeps out. But something always gets in. Henry sends him one of those damned labels. A fella like me walks through and where is he?" Grandfather's voice changed. He had resolved whatever had been bothering him. "Gentlemen, if you remember nothing else, remember this; everything has got a story. It's like the glue that holds things together. It's like guy wires or spiderwebs or telephone lines. Everything has got a story, and that is what holds the show together." He had started using his tour-guide voice again, but my question was involuntary. I was thinking of the fence.

"Everything?"

"No question about it."

"What if you don't remember it right? What if everyone forgets?"

He looked down at me, but when he spoke he did not answer my question, but, I suspect, one of his own. "Well, gentlemen, if they start to forget then it's up to us to make them remember. What do you say Bob? Sounds to me like he is ready for Main Street."

Bobby, who in some way must have understood all of his life about stories and who must have known it was not just a matter of talking fast and well, smiled and nodded.

We finally made it to Main Street. We stepped out to see how the show was holding together, to check out just what kind of shop they had been running, to promenade, to cake-walk, to see, be seen, talk, listen, to view the latest rage and watch the passing of spent fashion; whatever else he did for me that summer, my grandfather educated me in the phenomena known as Main Street, and I cannot think of it without hearing the cadences of his voice. "Boys, Main Street is not measured in feet and inches. Main Street is as long as Saturday night when you are sixteen years old. It's as long as Sunday afternoon when you are 75. It's as long as the week you spent to get there, gentlemen, and it's taller than any other street in town because it is the one street where you perform the miracle of looking up after a week of staring at your feet with that weekday crimp in your neck. It's the widest street in the world because when you look across it you never know who or what you will see. The world is a conversation, my friends, and Main Street is where the talking gets done."

"Step up, boys, step up and straighten out," is all he said that first day. Looking long to the left and long to the right, he shook his head and smiled. "Main Street, boys, Main Street," and amazement and amusement were mixed in his face and voice.

We cross-stitched Main Street that day, back and forth, back and forth. As the day wore on, my attention began to disperse and gather in unlikely places. In Swartz's butcher shop all that I noticed was a fly that worried endlessly over a pile of sawdust, rising and settling, rising and settling, knowing there was blood in the shavings but unable to reach it. In the mossy coolness of the pool hall I was caught by the careless angles of the cues and the men bent over the tables. In the *Union Chronicle* print shop the stroboscopic movement of the Heidelburg press back and forth behind the railing that separated the shop from the office hypnotized me. Standing in the shadows and looking across to the sunny side of the street, I noticed how the heat and dust smudged and softened the edges of the shadows. Standing on the sunny side and looking at the false-front buildings on the other side I would squint so that the scene would flatten out as if it were a painted backdrop, fall back into perspective, only to flatten out once more as if it were moving in and out with my breath.

The longer the shadows grew that day, the younger I felt. It was much like when I was four or five years old and folllowing my mother around on an interminable afternoon shopping-trip. I would begin by trying to look up and around at everything, but by the late afternoon I would give up and simply focus in on the click of her high heels and the forest of legs around me. I would be stumbling along with her when I would begin to see through the myriad of nylon and trouser-clad legs what amounted to apparitions: the drunkards sitting on curbs, the cripples, the Skate Board Man and all of the others, who for one reason or another, lived down at my four-year-old level of the world.

There was one apparition, however, which frightened me far more than any of the others, even the Skate Board Man. It was a boy who stood on the corner of Eighth Avenue and Third Street where we caught the bus to go home. I saw him every shopping-trip, and because of him I came to dread going home. It was impossible to say how old he was, but he could not have been more than ten. It was his face that disturbed me. The upper half of it, his nose and eyes and forehead, was completely relaxed and expressionless, as if he was unconscious or sleeping. His eyes, however, were open, and they continually moved back and forth over the passing crowd. His body was as relaxed as the upper part of his face. He held the daily paper across his chest. But in the space between the stillness of his body and the stillness of his upper face was a disconnected and deeply disturbing movement. His mouth was opened wide. From out of it came a piercing, nasal sound. EEEEEEEvnning PAAAAAAperrrrrr, EEEEEEEvnning PAAAAAAperrrrrr. The sound was inhuman and it rang out even over the traffic noise. In other circumstances I might have been impressed by such an ability, but the roiling, slack-jawed movement of his mouth was in such an aborted relationship with the stillness of the rest of his body and face that it struck me with complete terror. It was explained to me that he was calling the way he did simply in order to sell papers, but the explanation made it worse. People like the Skate Board Man had no choice in how they were, but here was someone not too much older than myself who willingly contorted himself. I refused to be convinced that it was acceptable.

Then, on Main Street, just when I was feeling most like a five-year-old kept up beyond his afternoon nap, I once more began to encounter apparitions. It was appropriate that the first one I met reminded me of the paper boy. We met Helen Stadler in front of the bank. At first glance she seemed completely mundane. It was not until she spoke that I became disconcerted.

"Well, Mr. Caldwell, how nice it is to see you once again. I was just saying to Gerald this morning at breakfast that I thought perhaps one of Union's most venerable citizens had taken ill." She spoke as if mentally punctuating her sentences, but what was even more unsettling was that she used the same sort of inflated rhetoric that Grandfather occasionally employed. The difference was that Mrs. Stadler had none of my grandfather's ironic tone; instead she pronounced the words with a kind of satisfaction and seemed very careful to remember to close her mouth after speaking.

"Well, Helen, it's always nice to know I have been missed."

"Indeed you have, Mr. Caldwell, indeed you have." She paused, and then she seemed to almost swivel, moving her shoulders and head, to look at me. "And this must be your grandson, the young man who is the talk of the town today." Her face changed from solicitude for my grandfather to friendly welcome for me, but it was not convincing. She used her facial expressions with the same exactitude as she punctuated her sentences. I was immediately reminded of Marion Barker, a girl who lived across the alley from me in the city. Marion had developed a large number of ways of dressing and using her hands in order to hide a birthmark on her neck, but the effect of all her subterfuges was always to call attention to her neck. Helen Stadler used her facial expressions the same way, but I could not understand what she was trying to hide. Later in the summer Bobby remarked that she had ice in her face, and that was it exactly. For all its apparent mobility her face created the same confusion as the first skim of ice over a pond or puddle; the surface seems natural enough, but there is no real animation.

When I quit staring at her and began to listen to my grandfather once more, he was just finishing his spiel about what he was doing with Bobby and me. He had been polishing it all day, and it was turning into quite a production. "...so the way I figure it, it is my task, the duty of my age and experience, as it were, to pass on to these boys the tricks of the trade." I was later to realize he always became slightly more verbose when faced with Helen Stadler.

"Good for you, Mr. Caldwell. Good for you. Still, from what I hear, Jonathan is already quite a capable little man." She swivelled toward me. "It was very heroic of him to stand by Jennifer Scott's young Bobby. Wayne, Patrick and the others are simply buzzing about it."

Perhaps I had offended or even threatened her by staring. Perhaps she did not think I understood what she meant when she said that Wayne and Patrick were "simply buzzing." Or perhaps, although it was rare in my experience with adults, Helen Stadler was being clearly and deliberately malicious. Grandfather was trying to smooth the whole thing over with "boys will be boys" and other similar expressions, but she refused to let it go. Raising her voice slightly she spoke over him. "Still, I must confess, I do not understand what all of the fuss is about. The Scott boy certainly does not look much worse for the wear."

I saw Grandfather sharpen slightly. He did not like to be shushed or ignored. "Well Helen, I guess that is the resiliency of youth." He paused. "But who knows, if Jonathan here had panicked and taken off with the others, it might not have ended so well."

Mrs. Stadler was not in the least fazed. Her face became concerned, and then she spoke. "You are absolutely right, Mr. Caldwell. The whole episode could have ended tragically, but I am reluctant to think that any of the boys who were there were at fault. There are many people in this town who are, quite sincerely, worried that the Scott girl has too much to do already. She is after all, a very busy young woman. What with her many activities at the hotel all day and trying to look after Bobby without the benefit of a steadying father figure, some people think that he would be much better off with professional care and instruction." She closed her mouth very carefully. There was silence. It suddenly seemed that her final comment had been the one she was intending to make all along. I looked at Bobby. He had become perfectly still. Grandfather was looking off down the street. It was completely deserted in the mid-afternoon heat. When he spoke it was as if his voice was coming from a distance.

"You know I think you are right. Jennifer Scott works pretty hard. In fact I think she works a lot harder than most people in this town. So, I guess you will be pleased to know that I have agreed to keep an eye on these two boys this summer. All those people you say are so concerned about the situation can relax a little bit. I figure he will be good company for my grandson. Good for me too. It should provide me with a fresh point of view. We can all use a fresh point of view once in a while, Helen."

"It is very civic-minded of you Mr. Caldwell, I'm sure. But I don't think we could really call your help professional, could we? Besides, isn't it a rather temporary measure?"

"One of the things I have learned is that most things are temporary. You learn that when you become, as you say, a venerable citizen." He paused. "Yep. I figure most things are temporary. So I guess I will take a temporary solution if I can find one. After all, the problem could be temporary too, couldn't it? Kind of sharp of you to point that out." He had begun to smile.

To give her credit, she came back with the best she had, but it was weak and she knew it. "Well, it will be nice for you, anyways, Mr. Caldwell. So many of our older citizens just don't know what to do with themselves when they retire. Well, I really must be hurrying along. I have things to do, and I certainly can't afford to stand here on the street and talk, pleasant as it is. Be sure to give my best to Ruby." She was turning to go.

"You can depend on me Helen." She paused in confusion, her face momentarily uncertain about its expression. "To give Ruby your best," he explained. "You can depend on me. Now you just hurry along. You must have important things to do."

All three of us were silent as we watched her move off down the street. I do not think that Bobby or I could have been thinking much beyond how we were suddenly feeling very tired, but my grandfather must have had some inkling of what had taken place.

When he finally did speak, it was an attempt to repair the damage she had done to our day. "Funny thing about people like Helen Stadler, boys. You could take a rose to her with the best intentions, and ten minutes later you would wonder if you were really trying to get her with a thorn."

Bobby became unthawed. "That's not true about my mother. She takes good care of me. She is not too busy to take good care of me."

"Don't worry about it Bob. Mrs. Stadler is just a bit confused about the word busy. I figure she has got the notion that anyone who is not wearing a black-and-white checked dress and doesn't have the initials H.S. is bound to be doing something that she might not approve of. As a view of life it has an elegant simplicity. I should imagine it gets a bit frustrating though. Anyways boys, we might as well trim the sails and get back on course. It looks like I have signed the three of us up for the summer, and barring objections from Jennifer, I figure we are going to have to plan out our campaign."

Two hours later found us sitting on benches in front of the hotel. We were in the shade, but the heat was bouncing up at us from the street. Grandfather had just finished informing Wesley Stoller of the things he planned to do with us that summer. Because Mr. Stoller was very hard of hearing, he had inadvertently informed anyone passing by as well. It was, I suppose, very considerate of Grandfather to insure that Mr. Stoller understood the details of what Grandfather called "the campaign," but four o'clock in the afternoon of a long and hot day is not the right time to listen to someone shout out a list of relatively preposterous activities.

To this day, I am convinced he developed his list from the Norman Rockwell-type prints he had on the kitchen wall. I also suspect he had a number of others tucked away somewhere, because as well as fishing, kite flying and swimming in forbidden swimming-holes, he had a number of other visions on the order of stealing still-warm apple pies from window ledges where they had been set to cool, writing initials in still-wet cement and flattening pennies on the railroad tracks. He had only had two hours to develop his material, and the necessity of shouting to Mr. Stoller prohibited him from embellishing each item in a proper fashion. He reached firmer ground when he was able to move into a dissertation on benches, a topic that he had obviously laboured over many times.

"You know boys, I figure a bench on Main Street is just about the best place for a bench. Bench in a park is all right. Sure. Feed the pigeons. Look at other people feeding pigeons. Not quite my cup of tea, but I guess it has its points. I figure the bench we got down at the railroad station is all right too. They got a machine down there now that sells coffee. The view is good too. Far as that goes, if it's a view you want, I remember the year I worked on a road out west of Lakeview in the Mountains. I was out there for a month and a half after seeding. The bunkhouse looked straight on Mount Bronson and there was a bench out front. That damned mountain changed every day of the week. Weather on it, snow pulling back, change of colour, change of cloud. That was one of the best sit-downs in my whole life. Yessir I'll take a bench just about anywhere, but a bench on Main Street is about the best there is."

He turned to Mr. Stoller. "WESLEY...WESLEY... I FIGURE A BENCH ON MAIN STREET IS DOING ALL RIGHT. YOU HAVE HAD IT FIGURED OUT FOR A FEW YEARS NOW, HAVEN'T YOU?" Mr. Stoller smiled, nodded and continued to chew whatever he was chewing. Grandfather turned back to us, "I try and include old Wesley here whenever I can. He is a pretty good old man. Mind you, he has been working on it for a while now. Count up the years and he is not that many ahead of me, but he has been practising since he was 40. I figure he has got it down pat. They say if you want to find a good roadside café that you look for where the truckers stop. Well, if you want to find the best bench you look for some old son of a bitch like Wesley here who hasn't done much for the last 40 years, because you know he'll have his tent pegged down where the water's close and the sun is warm. He knows his business.... I WAS JUST SAYING WESLEY THAT YOU HAVE PROBABLY SEEN IT ALL SITTING HERE? RIGHT?"

Mr. Stoller made motions with his mouth that were slightly different than the chewing movements he had made up to that point, and then he actually began to speak. "I've seen it hotter I guess. Folks seem to like to talk about the weather a lot, but I guess the sun will shine anyways."

"SURE IT WILL WESLEY. YOU ARE DEAD RIGHT ABOUT THAT." Mr. Stoller nodded wisely.

I was tired of it all. I knew that Grandfather had just hit

his stride about benches, and I felt the beginnings of irritability. Perhaps it was simply the cumulative effect of the day, or perhaps it was even something physical like the hot stuffy feeling before a thunderstorm. Grandfather continued to expound on benches. It was almost as if he knew that Bobby and I were slipping away on him, and he was determined that we hear it all. It reminded me of school visits to art galleries. By the time we reached the last roomful of pictures, the teacher would be exhorting the class more than speaking to it, and each one of us would be rebelling in our own particular way. Some would giggle, some would shove and some would make repeated trips to the washroom or water fountain. Most of us went into a kind of dull-eyed holding pattern that was completely impervious to the most Rubenesque nude. For many of my companions I think the substance of their reverie was largely daydreams, but with me it was a kind a catatonic withdrawal.

Resting my head on my hands, I drew my feet up on the bench, and in a posture like the monkey that hears no evil, I stared wearily out at the street. Fragments of what my grandfather was saying became mixed up with what I saw there.

"...I figure if you spend enough time sitting here, a day would seem just like a smoke ring, there and gone again, just that quick." A breeze came up and a sheet of newspaper bounded into my field of view, flattened itself out against the street, then leapt up and away again. "...maybe like a river. Never step in the same one twice. Just sit here long enough and let the world float by." The hanging General Store sign across the street began to swing back and forth. "Slap the paint on and then watch it peel. Watch the snow fall. Watch it melt. Yep. Yep, the whole show is right out there in front of you..." I suddenly wondered about the peeling, dissolving fence. Maybe everything was like that. Appearing and disappearing. I clasped my arms around my knees. I noticed a bruise on my right hand just before the knuckles. I had bruised it the night I had arrived in Union trying to open the basement window. Already it had faded and was barely distinguishable from the blue vein on the back of my hand. It shocked me that it was still there and it shocked me that it was fading. In only a few days it would be gone. "I figured it out once. You figure a hundred people pass down this street a day. You figure 30,000 a year. Twenty years makes a half a million journeys. All in the blink of an eye..." It seemed I could hear a rustling and susurration around me. "...and before that I guess it would be the Cree and before that who knows. Maybe ocean waves. Yep. In geologic terms it is all spit on a hot skillet. It shines and goes, shines and goes." But I could still hear the rustle and the whisper, like static on a radio or far-off applause. Or like grains of sand blowing against a window-pane.

It was grains of sand. A dust devil suddenly materialized in front of the hotel and stung me awake. It might have brought everything back into perspective but for what I suddenly saw across the street. Standing behind the right-hand display window of the hardware store, his arms crossed, was George Maclenan. It seemed he was staring directly at me. I suppose he could have been looking anywhere, but standing as he was, he was like one of those gargoyles that seem to look in every direction at once. I am not even sure how I knew it was George Maclenan. I suppose it must have been the fact that there was only one person in the hardware, and that meant it had to be him, but I did not go through any such logical process to arrive at my conclusion. I simply knew it was him. I had a sudden conviction that he had appeared from inside the dust devil, and I felt a further conviction that he was somehow looking directly into the back of my mind and all the confusion that was there. He was impassive about it, faceless behind the window, and he fascinated me. I could not help but stare back at him. Grandfather had been re-lighting his cigar, but suddenly, because he had noticed me staring, or because he had seen George

Maclenan for himself, he began speaking in a quiet bitter voice that confirmed my anxiety about the figure in the window. For a moment it seemed that we had all been waiting for the meeting to occur.

"Damn. The man might as well advertise that he has got no business. Standing there like a cigar-store Indian, he might as well run an ad in the *Chronicle* telling people to come down and strike a match on his nose. Damn. You want to know about stories, listen to the one he is tellng right now. He is telling the whole damn town that he has got no business, and from there it's only a small step before people start figuring there is a reason he has got no business. Then where is he gonna be. Bullshit is what the man said. Well it comes home now, doesn't it. He should be using a bit of bullshit right now or he is gonna get himself in trouble, and if he wasn't so pigheaded I would go over and tell him. Gawddamn. A fella doesn't want to buy an axe handle. He wants to hear about the oak they cut down for it. He wants to hear about how when a big tree goes down the water pumps up from the stump like blood from an artery. Saturday in town and a fella wants to hear a story. He wants something he can take out onto that field all day with him that isn't gonna make just another callus." Grandfather was shaking his head in disgust and, I think, confusion. He stood up.

"C'mon boys. If I stick around here any longer I am gonna get myself in trouble. We got one more stop to make."

What Grandfather was saying made sense to me even then. But now I wonder if it was true. Now I wonder if George Maclenan standing behind his display window was not serving as some sort of Rorschach ink blot. In him I saw an impassive, faceless approval of the carousel of changes I had been faced with all spring. I think my grandfather saw the beginnings of what he felt was going wrong with Union and his world in general. In the final analysis, it may have been Bobby's vision of George Maclenan that was the truest.

That day, as we moved west down Main Street he stopped for a moment, turned, looked back and then spoke, "He looks lonely."

I chanced a look myself. He did.

There was only one more apparition that day, or perhaps vision would be a better word. Tessa Maclenan was the last main character in the story of that summer. It seems to me now that as we trekked down Main Street and then out across the baseball diamond on the west end of town Grandfather was silent. This seems highly unlikely, so it could be I had simply stopped hearing him speak. Indeed, it seems I remember very little of that part of the journey. Bobby and I might have been close to sunstroke. I could feel the dry heat on the back of my neck and on my nose that comes along with sunburn. Bobby looked worse than I felt. If it is possible to look more red and more pale at the same time, that is how he looked.

Then suddenly I woke up. We were on a small road that ran through the stand of poplars on the far side of the baseball diamond. Actually it was more like two paths running side by side with a ridge of grass in the middle. There was just the faintest breeze, not enough to rustle the leaves, but it produced that minimal, inexpressible sound that comes just before the rustling that is so faint that you are not sure if it is a sound or perhaps a smell. There was also a number of distinct smells: the watermelon scent of moist earth, grass, ferns and flowers was saved from overripeness by the acerbic smell of poplars. The ground was dappled with sunlight, but now the shadows were faintly green and not the warm brown of Main Street.

I was stopped dead, right on the pathway, and Bobby and Grandfather were stopped as well, looking back at me. Bobby was smiling, and I knew that he knew what was happening to me. Grandfather seemed about to speak when we heard another voice. It seemed to come out of the trees and

151

air around us.

"Twenty-two...23...24...25...I have ears...a plentitude ...but I haven't any feet...although I have no mouth...all I taste is sweet...31...32...Do you give up?...34...Corn, stupid...I have more eyes than anyone...I see beneath the earth...although I'm very humble...even Kings concede my worth...40...41...42..."

Another voice broke into the counting. "Well, what is it?"

The counting voice continued. "You figure it out...44..."

"Come on you guys, let's go back to the rink. It's a stupid game anyways." There was a short pause. "And no girls allowed."

"Who cares 45.... Who cares 46...."

Wayne Maclenan, Patrick Stadler and Raymond Hueffer appeared from around the curve ahead of us. I had dreaded meeting them all day because I knew they would be prepared to be derisive at the very least. But as on the day before, they did not see us until they were upon us. Wayne's surprise combined with his undignified retreat from whoever was counting and reciting poetry completely diffused the situation. He looked up at us first with shock and then dismay. Then he and the other two boys pedalled furiously past us.

We walked around the curve in the track. It opened up into a small clearing. The first thing I saw was a small structure on the far side. I thought it was some sort of thatched cottage or treehouse. I could tell it was a man-made structure, but bushes and vines and flowers had grown round it and under it and over it. Then I saw that it had two large metal wheels on either side, and I think the thought crossed my mind that it was some sort of covered, medicine-show waggon of the kind I had read about and seen in movies. The owner of the counting voice was moving smoothly up and down behind the railing, almost as if she were being raised and lowered by pulleys. She appeared and disappeared in cadence with the counting. The sight was so surprising I might have discounted it as a heat mirage, but Grandfather was smiling up at the girl so I knew she must be real.

"Well, young lady, I figured there could only be one person up here reciting poetry."

"Hi Mr. Caldwell 49." She disappeared again. Then she reappeared. "Fifty. I'm practising my ballet." She stood still and looked straight down at us.

"Yes, that's what I figured. I am willing to bet that you were only supposed to do 25 of those knee bends."

She smiled. "Thirty, and they are called demi-pliés."

"Well, whatever they are called, I guess this means you have given up on being a waitress. I was kind of looking forward to ordering a cup of coffee and a piece of pie from you."

"You would be apple, wouldn't you?"

"Yep. That is what I would be, young lady. A la mode, I guess. Seems to me the world has lost a good waitress even before she started."

"Not necessarily. I intend to sling hash until I am established as a ballet dancer."

My grandfather threw back his head and laughed outright. I looked on with amazement, not so much at her as at the combination of her and my grandfather. She was not much older than I was, but she was dealing with my grandfather with perfect aplomb. She was at least as comfortable with him as Mr. Barstow.

"You have been talking with someone, young lady. I hear the echo in your voice, but I am not quite sure who it is. Joe down at the café?"

"No. When I said I wanted to be a waitress, you told me I better talk to someone in the business. So I did. I talked to Bobby's mother." She paused, and then did something only Mr. Barstow had done that day. "Hello Bobby."

He smiled happily. "Hello Tessa."

"Jennifer told me if I wanted to sling hash she would let me try it for a few days. She said that when my arms started to feel like they were going to drop off I would change my mind."

"Somehow I doubt it."

"I'm doing pushups, and Jennifer will be surprised. I can already beat my brother."

"I would be interested to know what your mother thinks of your aspirations. My guess is that she would consider them less than feminine."

"Aspirations? You mean the pushups?"

"Same thing I guess."

"She thinks I am doing them to develop my bustline and she approves."

Grandfather actually began to guffaw, and I realized that it was the first time I had ever seen him be content to simply provide the straight lines. He was so taken with her that for the first time that day he neglected to introduce me and go into his spiel about passing on his experience to the younger generation. When he had finished laughing, she asked him outright.

"Is that your grandson?"

"It is indeed, and I have been dilatory in my introductions. You can look up dilatory when you look up aspiration. Jonathan meet Union's one and only ballerina, she sits a better horse than most men I have seen, and if and when she gets around to it, she will sling a meaner hash than anyone this side of Montreal. In short, meet Tessa Maclenan."

"Pleased to meet you Jonathan. My little brother is a jerk, and he should be boiled in oil. I am glad you are all right Bobby."

I could not think of a thing to say. Grandfather smiled at me and spoke. "Well Tessa, looks to me like you have made a conquest. He's speechless."

I finally found my voice. "Potatoes." All three of them looked at me with surprise. "Potatoes. That's the answer to your poem. Potatoes."

"That's right. Do you like puzzle poems?"

154

I nodded.

"Good. So do I. I have to go now. It's soufflé night and Mother gets really upset." She scissored over the railing and dropped to the ground in one motion "Goodbye Mr. Caldwell. I missed you that last little while. Goodbye Jonathan. Bye Bobby." She turned and walked off. At the edge of the clearing she stopped and called back. "I know lots more. Do you?"

"Yes. Yes I do." And I did. I knew dozens of them. She turned and disappeared around the bend.

Everything had become just fine once again. I wondered why I had started to become so cross back on Main Street. The summer opened up for me once more. We turned and continued out to the hill overlooking the Sortie River valley.

As we stepped out of the poplars and on to the brow of the hill it was as if the world was providing me with an expanded exterior view to match the expansion in my mental landscape. The Sortie River ran below us, roughly north by northwest. Union was perched on the south and east side almost overlooking the valley. From the hill we had a good view both up and down the valley. I could see where the road crossed the river, and Grandfather pointed out where the airplane had attempted to land so many years before. Looking down at Rose's pasture, I felt a sense of ownership. Downriver, closer to where we were standing, the railroad tracks crossed the river on a wooden trestle. From where we were it looked a bit like a piece of playground apparatus or a mechano toy. The trestle disappeared into the trees on the farther side, which at that point came right down to the river's edge.

There was something special about the hillside. Perhaps it was seeing the purple distance of the horizon or perhaps it was the breeze that was stronger on the valley's edge than it had been in the poplars, but I felt a settling in my shoulders and back as if some tension had just left me. Grandfather's voice seemed less loud, and in the context of the long, rustling grass of the hillside, Bobby's slight waverings were unnoticeable. The sun was lowering, and it shone off the river. We made our way over to a rough log bench that had been built on the hillside.

We sat down on the bench, Grandfather at one end, me at the other and Bobby in the middle. For a while it seemed we just smelled the breeze, and then Grandfather began to speak.

"I guess I have led you fellas on a bit of a chase today. Ruby will not approve, but what the hell, this is the last stop. I made it myself. It's funny. Everyone in town probably uses it once in a while, but whenever I come out here it seems like my secret." He stretched out his legs and crossed them at the ankle. "I use this place like a barometer." He looked over at me. "Like Hansel and Gretel and the Witch." He meant the little house that sat on the refrigerator; when the children were out it was going to be mild, but when the witch was out it meant stormy weather.

"When I was in the store, some days were like shipping cartons, and you got to feeling like the shredded paper they use for packing. And the funny thing was the slower the day the more tired you felt. You have to be careful with a day like that. It's like poison, and it can ruin you for two weeks." He looked over at us again, and I wondered how close I had been to having such a day.

"Well anyways, I'd come out here after a day like that and sooner or later whatever was in the back of my head would move forward. On a bad day I would find myself swung around to the west just like I was a weather-vane. I would just sit and stare at the sun going down, and do you know what I would be thinking about after one of the bad ones? Mountains. 'The soul that travels west will win his hour of sun, and if he travels well enough, his day is never done.' It's true. All of your big migrations go west. So I would come out here after a day of tap-dancing around that store all day, and I would think about mountains. It wasn't ever the money I worried about. The money was always pretty good. There weren't any chain-stores to volume-buy you out of business, but it wasn't money that I really wanted anyways. It was something else. You know what I think I wanted? I think I wanted every one of those people who stepped into that store to hear something they had never heard before. I wanted to make them jump if they were standing still. I wanted to freeze them if they were moving too fast. Damn. It was that change I wanted. Like wind on the slough. One minute grey as slate and the next shining like butter on a skillet. It was that change I wanted.

"But some days it didn't happen. Some days I'd try for it and miss it and then it was like my clothes didn't fit. It wasn't like tripping over your own feet out in the field with nobody but the crows to caw, no sir. You knew damn well that before the day was out people would be talking about that crazy Rod Caldwell. So I would come out here and stare west until I could feel the ice in the wind. Mountains. Blue ice, green ice. I've worked in them, and I have travelled through them. Up there they have passes where no-one has ever been. Make your tracks in one of those valleys and they would be the first a man's ever made there. Think about it boys."

I was thinking about it. I had closed my eyes, and I was probably waving in the wind like Bobby. The breeze washed over me in waves. I could see the shadowed, glacier-ringed valley.

"Can you see it Jonathan?" I opened my eyes. Grandfather was looking at me and smiling. I spoke without thinking.

"It's like Uncle John's picture, isn't it?"

His gaze slipped away from me and out to the distance. "Yep. I guess you are right at that. You were always kind of partial to that picture, weren't you. Can't say that I have ever been comfortable with it myself. Ruby had to hang it though." The expression that had been starting in his face left, and he straightened up on the bench and looked over his shoulder. "But turn yourselves around. Most times I come out here I find myself turned around and staring back at town."

Behind us, perhaps a quarter of a mile back from the valley's edge, we could see the outline of Union, its grain elevators poking up like three smoke stacks in the middle and the jumble of trees and bushes and houses banking off to either side.

"Yep. It was from right about here that I first saw it. Road cut used to be just below us. We had been looking at property all that fall. Over in Bellam, Skylar, Long Valley, everywhere but our own back door. I've often wondered how it would have been if we'd gone for Bellam. I'd pretty well made up my mind for it, but Ruby wasn't happy about it. I think she thinks that is why we ended up here, closer to the homestead, but that wasn't it. It was that night I saw it, I mean really saw it, for the first time. We were coming back about eight in the evening. The sky was still light in the west, but over Union it was moonrise. I looked out the window, and there it was like I had never seen it before. I had to pull over. My cousin Marvin used to work the fishing-boats all the way down the eastern seaboard. When I was a boy he told me that when one of those big passenger liners went by at night it was like the city of God. That is what he said, just like the city of God, nothing to say how big, nothing to say how small, just a blaze of light running by in the night. That is how Union looked that night. Oh I guess it wasn't much light by today's standards, but back then they didn't splash it around like they do now.

"A fella once told me, and I have read it since, that they have everything you'd ever need. You name it, cafés, libraries, repair shops, movie houses. Why, I guess they even have stores. Who knows, maybe a bit of hardware. And that is what she looked like that night boys, like the city of God sailing over the brow of the hill, full moon on the rise behind her. I knew right then that she had everything I needed. Lately I have been getting the feeling she is a bit off course..." He shook his head, not in negation, but in wonder. "But it's still all there. Gawddamn, it's still all there." When Bobby and I turned back from looking at Union he was standing up, looking down at us.

"Well gentlemen, you should have the picture now. What'll it be? West to the mountains or East to Babylon?" Bobby and I exchanged glances, then he swung back toward Union.

"I reckon you're right Bob. What the hell, we got the whole summer to get her back on course."

Bobby looked up at him and spoke. He tried for Grandfather's cadence and delivery, but he was slightly off and it came out both profound and comical. "Well Mr. Caldwell, I figure a whole summer is all the time in the world."

Grandfather started laughing. "By gawd, I never had any trouble being young, and you two make me remember why." Still laughing he started back toward town. The day seemed to find a final point of balance in his laughter, and I paused, savouring it. Then I turned west, thinking for a moment that if I stared hard enough I could look beyond the horizon and catch a glimpse of the far mountains. Before Bobby and Grandfather had gone too far, they noticed I was lagging behind. They called for me to catch up. I turned and walked toward them and Union.

So, the summer had begun. I am reminded of the old child's song about cause and effect.

> There was an old woman
> Who swallowed a dog.
> What a hog, to swallow a dog.
> She swallowed the dog to catch the cat.
> She swallowed the cat to catch the bird.

She swallowed the bird to catch the spider
That wiggled and jiggled and tickled inside her.
She swallowed the spider to catch the fly.
I don't know why she swallowed the fly.
Perhaps she'll die.

I had come to Union looking for the lights that had once danced for me in the forest, but as I walked toward town that afternoon, the image I had was my grandfather's city of God, blazing with light and sailing into the darkness. I had signed on as his apprentice in storytelling. Only a few days later I would begin to narrate to Bobby the story of the Lonely Elk and the Western Kingdom, and in nightly episodes we would follow the adventures of our counterparts in that Kingdom, Wolfsbane and Foxglove. Before the summer was over, they would lead Bobby, Tessa and me far, far beyond the lights of Union.

All of the seeds had been planted.